DANCING

WITH

LANGSTON

✦

DANCING
WITH
LANGSTON

✦

A NOVEL

SHARYN SKEETER

GREEN PLACE BOOKS *Brattleboro, Vermont*

Printed in the United States

10 9 8 7 6 5 4 3 2 1

Green Writers Press is a Vermont-based publisher whose mission is to spread a message of hope and renewal through the words and images we publish. Throughout, we will adhere to our commitment to preserving and protecting the natural resources of the earth. To that end, a percentage of our proceeds will be donated to environmental activist groups and The Southern Poverty Law Foundation. The author will make a special donation to *Seattle Inspiring Connections Outdoors* (ICO), part of the Seattle Group of the Sierra Club. Green Writers Press gratefully acknowledges support from individual donors, friends, and readers to help support the environment and our publishing initiative. Green Place Books curates books that tell literary and compelling stories with a focus on writing about place—these books are more personal stories/memoir and biographies.

GREEN
PLACE
BOOKS

GReen
wriTers
press

Giving Voice to Writers & Artists Who Will Make the World a Better Place
Green Writers Press | Brattleboro, Vermont
www.greenwriterspress.com

ISBN: 978-1-9505841-9-2

COVER DESIGN BY ASHA HOSSAIN DESIGN, LLC
COVER & FRONTISPIECE IMAGE: ALAMY

For

Irma Langston Skeeter

and Clarence Doyle Skeeter

✦

You have to dance unencumbered. There's no other way to move. The idea of dance is freedom. It is not exclusiveness, it's inclusiveness.

—JUDITH JAMISON

✦

We have a choice. We can spend our whole life suffering because we can't relax with how things really are, or we can relax and embrace the open-endedness of the human situation, which is fresh, unfixated, unbiased.

—PEMA CHODRON

DANCING

WITH

LANGSTON

✦

CHAPTER I

✦

THE JERK SAT with his fingers tapping on the meter, waiting for his tip.

"Lady! Look, I can't get the cab through. They got that truck blockin' the street. You gotta get outta here."

"Get out here? Are you kidding?"

This wasn't good for me, but he was right. There was no way into the side street, past the construction truck and parked cars. I had to lug out from the back seat the old blue suitcase and plaid carry-on that I'd brought for Cousin Ella's clothes.

When I got out on the corner, I fumbled in my purse to pull out Dad's letter. I needed to reread where he said I'd find Cousin Ella. I was on Lenox Avenue, standing under the scaffolding surrounding the buildings on the block. My heart raced when I heard the clunks of falling bricks above my head and I coughed from breathing old dust from busted walls. I skimmed to the end of Dad's letter—shaky handwriting on lined paper.

P.S. The pain is starting, but I'm not asking for morphine yet. With my fuzzy mind, I forgot to say where she lives. I can't even remember the street. The building is number 24, her apartment is 62. You'll find it in a side street directly across from those tall apartment buildings where Mr. Jackson lived.

I had to get my bearings. I had looked up Cousin Ella's address in the white pages, but I wanted to be sure. Facing east, the Harlem River was just beyond that housing complex of tall buildings across the street. Mr. Jackson, Dad's old Army war buddy, lived there when I was a young girl. Dad used to bring me when he'd go to see him. While the men would talk of the horrors they encountered at Dachau and the prejudice of some white officers, I would stand by the window and watch tugboats maneuver, synchronized, in the muddy water. Sometimes Dad would mumble about how his older cousin Langston gallivanted around the world while he put on a uniform and fought for his country—and life—in the Black Forest.

He also told me the Savoy Ballroom had been right across there on Lenox Avenue and 141st Street, and the Cotton Club had been nearby. I loved his stories of the jazzy dancers in the chorus line. I imagined myself in their short skirts as I tried out their dance steps in my bedroom. Cousin Ella had been one of those dancers before she went to Paris. Why did everything that was gone remind me of Dad?

But I had no time to sightsee. The bags were heavy and I had to find her place. I just had four hours to get the odds and ends of Cousin Ella's packing done. I had to be at the lawyer's office to sign away my condo to a Wall Street trader. He and his wife were excited about moving in. I heard him whisper to her that they were getting a deal at my asking price. I should have complained to the agent for lowering the price so much, but my husband, Bill, had wanted a quick sale.

"Hey, miss!" A young man in jeans yelled at me as he bopped out of a deli eating chips. He saw me struggling with the luggage and my purse. "You need help?"

"No, thank you."

"Oh, she must think she's too cute to talk to us," he said to his buddy who followed behind him, and they both laughed at me as they dipped and strolled away.

Cute? I was almost forty. That's not cute. I'd snipped out my first gray hairs last week. I wasn't ready for them.

With my purse and the carry-on hanging on my shoulders, I pulled the suitcase into the block, then halfway down the street past a newly renovated gated building until I reached number twenty-four, a wreck of a place with a bumpy sidewalk in front. There were a few construction workers wearing yellow hard hats who were off-loading blue pipes and boards from the truck and placing them near the curb. Large oily puddles from last night's rain blocked my way to the entrance.

Cousin Ella was being kicked out. The entire block was being gentrified. For now, these construction guys seemed to be marking time, moving slowly with their work, and telling jokes. I made my way around them and through the puddles, up a few cracked concrete stairs, and into the lobby. I thought they would stop me, but they just glanced my way as if I were another pipe or plank.

By then I was panting. I stopped to look around at what once must have been a lovely building. The lobby's walls and floors were dirt-streaked, tannish marble. The ornate moldings near the ceiling were pocked with chipped paint. The floor had ruts from a hundred or more years of shoes, boots, slippers walking back and forth to the stairs at the right of the elevator.

I checked Dad's letter again. I needed to be clear.

My dear daughter Carrie,
The hospice nurse just told me that I might be gone by next week. They are giving me meds to try to calm me, but I'm still anxious about asking you to do this. Before I go into a coma, I've got to ask you to do an urgent favor for Cousin Ella.

You probably don't remember her, but you've heard me speak of her. She visited us once when you were a toddler. She had just come back from Paris to live in Harlem. She got you to do a little dance with her.

Mom (rest her soul) didn't like Cousin Ella. You never got to know her because Mom wouldn't let her visit us again. She didn't want Cousin Ella near you. Mom thought she might corrupt you.

*But you've got to do this for her—for me! I want
you to take care of her.*

He was right. I'd forgotten about Cousin Ella until
last week when I was cleaning out his apartment
and found the folded letter in his nightstand. Maybe
Cousin Ella had forgotten about me, too. She might
think I was coming out of nowhere. Why would she
want me to help her?

Of course the elevator wasn't working. It was a
gaping cave with the outer door off and the car gone.
It smelled of rancid garbage. My footsteps and every
sound I made in that lobby echoed, as did voices, probably squatters. I'd have to walk up the stairs.

Just as I lugged myself and the bags to the first landing, my phone buzzed. My husband.

"Bill?"

I covered my right ear and moved the phone closer
to my left when Young MC's "Bust a Move" started
echoing from an open apartment.

"Yes, yes. I know we need to leave tomorrow. But I
just got here . . . no. I haven't seen her, not yet . . . OK.
I'll hurry . . . yes, I know. Tomorrow night, red-eye. I
know. Bye!"

Yes, I knew it. I'd hung up too abruptly. But he
really couldn't complain. He'd found an excuse not
to come with me to help. Before I'd left the condo,
he'd told me he had more work to do on his new
job papers and had business to take care of. He'd
be the first black employee in his department, and I
was proud of him that he got hired, but he'd gotten

that word on the same day that Dad had died. I'd been in no mood to celebrate anything.

I knew that Dad would have been happy about Bill's success. Dad always told me that Bill would make something of himself. As for Bill? He'd start his new dream job next week. Me? I'd be back to sending out resumes. I'd worked hard to get promoted, executive in charge of the development department, and I hadn't planned to deal with that job search stress for years. But the day before had been my last on the job. I gave it up.

Broken, detached doors were piled up on two floors. Old soda spills on landings were sticky under my sneakers. I promised myself to do for Cousin Ella what Dad asked. When Dad died, besides the cancer, he had heart failure. When I was younger, I worked out every day to stay fit, but sometimes, like when I found my heart racing as I climbed the stairs, I worried about my own health. But I made it—past the trash, rotting chicken wings, and a few haggard squatters on mattresses in open apartments without doors.

They had heard me on the phone. Two women in brown pullovers stared my way. A young boy wrapped in a blanket stuck out his tongue. He saw my bags and yelled, "You moving somewhere, miss? Wish I could."

A middle-aged woman in a tight blue sweater and bell-bottomed jeans yelled, "I know you!" That jarred me. I was sure I didn't know her.

Here it was just a few days after burying Dad up in Westchester and I had to deal with Cousin Ella—a relative who I only knew from family gossip. To

Mom, she was "Jezebel"—the shameless cabaret dancer. Mom said Cousin Ella was a hussy. I looked closely in the photograph for traces of hussyness, but all I saw was a happy woman. Next to Cousin Ella was a dapper man grinning with a monkey in a fedora on a leash with a flashy gemstone collar. He looked like a puppet on the man's shoulder. I didn't know why Cousin Ella made Mom so upset, but when I was a child, when Dad made his weekly trek from the Bronx apartment to Cousin Ella's Harlem place with a box of food and toiletries, I was left at home with Mom to sneak a peep at the photo of Cousin Ella—a very young, brown, smiling woman in a red, fringed dress dancing some hootchy-kootchy in a Parisian café. I'd been intrigued. But over the years, my fixation on Cousin Ella had faded. I'd been wrapped up in my marketing career—and Bill.

On the top fifth and sixth floors, the apartments still had doors. Number sixty-two, Cousin Ella's, was in the corner on the sixth floor, according to Dad's details. I stood at that landing to catch my breath and set down the bags to rest my arms. Then I took out the letter again, as I had several times a day for the past week. I unfolded it like an altar cloth.

I know that in a few weeks you're moving to Seattle with Bill. (He's a good provider and a credit to all of us. You're a lucky woman.) There's enough in my safety deposit box for you to move Ella to the assisted living place—you know the one—where your mom was in her last days.

Now everything is different. Cousin Ella can't stay where she is even though she's been there for maybe 40, 50 some years. We had good times at her place, and even sometimes Langston showed up.

She didn't have much then. I gave her whatever I could. No, your mother didn't like that, but she couldn't stop me.

I'm passing on now, so it's your turn. Cousin Ella is my blood. All I have left of the old people. All YOU have left.

She has a gift for you. It's something of value that I'm ashamed that I couldn't give you—and too afraid to give you myself. Carrie, I want this to make it right. I want you to be happy.

We've always been loyal to each other. Promise me you'll do this, so I can go in peace.

Your loving Dad

My eyes were getting heavy. But, no. I couldn't cry. I'd done enough of that during the past week. I wondered if my crying was for Dad or myself. I had to tighten my face, control the tears.

"Don't you know how to knock on a door?" A woman's high-pitched, raspy voice yelled at me.

I was stunned. Then I looked up and saw a tiny woman in the half-open doorway. She opened the door a crack more. The chain lock on the door was still attached above her eyes.

"I'm—"

"I know who you are. Carrie. Cousin Doyle's daughter. He showed me photos of you. Look, I'll let you in. But I tell you now. I'm not going anywhere. I. Am. Not. Moving. You get that?"

"But—"

"No buts. So . . . do you want to come in or stand out in that hall? I don't want to stand here forever letting in that stink."

She was right. The smells of molding food and pools of stagnant water from ceiling leaks were upsetting my stomach. She released the chain and opened the door fully.

She was nothing like the photo of the oval-faced, slim dancer in the red dress. She was a short woman in a baggy sunflowered housecoat. I saw, in the door's shadow, that her face had rounded. Her gray hair was in two long braids. Her hands looked like dry, weathered parchment. This was Jezebel—the cabaret dancer Mom feared?

When she let me in, the scent of old rose perfume was overpowering—and so was the living room. I felt like I had stepped into a time machine. It was dark because the window blinds were pulled down. I scanned the room. Every inch of wall was covered with photos, portraits, nightclub scenes, old show programs from black Paris and Harlem in the 1930s, '40s, and '50s. Bricktop, Josephine Baker, Cousin Ella herself, and Langston Hughes. All were framed and giddily smiling everywhere on the paint-cracked walls.

So, it looked like the family stories Dad told Mr. Jackson about Langston being a cousin must have been true. Langston's books were lined atop the ornate ivory and gold-painted breakfront against the

back wall. Kitschy, chipped coffee mugs with his photo
were on a tray on a scratched wood table in the middle
of the room. Langston Hughes. Dad's cousin, Cousin
Ella's, and I guess mine, too. But at home, when I was
a girl, Dad went silent whenever I dared to mention
his name, like when I was in middle school and had to
memorize his poem "The Negro Speaks of Rivers."
He'd been off from his shift that night. He'd helped
me with algebra. But then he shut down. He said he
didn't have the time to help me with that poem.

"Well, come in all the way. What are you standing
in the doorway for? Put those bags over there. We
won't be needing them."

Cousin Ella pointed to a space on the floor between
the breakfront and a faded yellow barrelback side
chair. I was glad to set the luggage down. My right
arm was aching from carrying the bags up the stairs.
She pointed again to a slightly deflated club chair.
When I sat, the leather seat cushion sank as if many
years of butts had worn it out.

I wished I had come with more than a suitcase
and a carry-on. I was all set to pack some slippers,
nightgowns, and sweaters—a few old lady dresses for
special dinners in the assisted living home. The building manager there told me that's all she'd need. But
how could I possibly pack all this? Just with a quick
scan I saw crystal wine glasses, the Tiffany lamp in
the corner (Was it real?), the gold-rimmed dinner
plates greasy with leftover barbecue. I saw piles of
who-knew-what along the side wall. No doubt there
were lots of valuables I couldn't leave behind for the

construction workers to pick through, or worse, to destroy when in a day or two they would crash in the door.

I remembered seeing a liquor store down the block. I could get boxes there. Oh, but I'd have to get them up the stairs! That, and pack all this.

"So what do you think? You think you can fit my home in that cramped little old folk's place you got for me? I told you I'm not moving. I can't."

She watched me as I ignored her. She couldn't stay. She had to know that.

I looked around the room more slowly. As I got used to the shadowy light, I began to see the yellows, greens, oranges, blues, and lavenders of some furnishings. They were faded, frayed, and dusty—most in need of repair. I felt a suffocating need for sunshine and fresh air. Then I looked at my phone: 9:30. I had until lunchtime to get her out of here. My head jerked up when she giggled like a young girl.

"You can't do it."

Was she playing me? If she kept that up, I would leave—my promise to Dad or not. I had no loyalty to her. Then she'd be just like the other squatters in the building. I visualized her hungry, her eyes glazed, sitting on a blanket on her scuffed parquet floor. I didn't want her to wish she had taken my offer to move her.

I walked around the room, assessing it. She had so much of value, and so much junk. It could take a few days just to sort it out. I moved closer to see the photos and art on the wall, and quickly, Cousin Ella turned toward me, full face.

I tripped on the bare worn space on the Persian carpet and fumbled to hold on to a chairback. I looked up and the stark light from the shadeless ginger-jar lamp in the corner confirmed what I had seen. It was brutal. A topography of dark peaks and valleys on Cousin Ella's right cheek. I caught myself staring at the ridges of angry flesh. She caught me. She smirked.

I was embarrassed. But I wasn't sure if it was for her or me. I jerked away to look at the neat rows of framed art on the wall behind the frayed maroon sofa. Small canvases. Jacob Lawrence, Lois Mailou Jones. Photos. James Van Der Zee. In the center, a larger autographed photo of Langston Hughes. Precious pieces I'd need to pack.

I looked up at her again. Her smirk was gone.

"Baby, it's OK. Everyone who sees me stares. Some worse than you. Some young boys had the nerve to call me ugly. Other women said, 'Too bad. She'd have such a pretty face.' I knew they didn't mean it. They thought I was ugly. Made them think they were prettier. They weren't. They had that glue from those fake eyelashes all gummed up on their eyelids. I didn't need that. Still don't. I got long, pretty lashes. Don't you think?"

I focused on her eyes. They were light brown with green flecks. She still did have long, thick lashes.

I paused, then managed to say, softly, "Yes, they're pretty."

The smells of cloying rose perfume and stale barbecue sauce were making me queasy.

"You don't want to ask me about this?" She pointed to her scars.

I was silent, still taken by the look of them. I wanted to turn away but I couldn't. I stared at her. Smooth brown skin on most of her face. Surprisingly few wrinkles for a woman in her nineties. Salt-and-pepper hair with bed lint stuck on the scarred side. She was smiling with her lovely, bow-shaped lips. She pointed at me.

"You're funny, you know. You don't say much. But from those suitcases you brought, I know you want me outta here."

I didn't think I, or anything about this situation, was amusing. I heard my clipped, precise business voice. "That's why I'm here. They're tearing up this building. This apartment is condemned. I've made arrangements for you to go to a good place—"

"What place? An old folk's home to die?" She was getting more strident as she held the back of the sofa to steady herself.

"You'd have everything you'd need there."

I remembered the tour that the manager had given me. An adequately furnished studio apartment, meals, snacks, meds.

"You and Doyle want to cram me into one room. You want to feed me cardboard meals. Honey, you don't get it, do you? I need my space."

"It's a nice assisted-living studio apartment. Nice people. Good food. Your meds are taken care of. Most of all, it doesn't have ceiling leaks or roaches."

I saw her look furtively toward the leak in the kitchen ceiling.

"I don't need medicine. I don't want 'nice.' This is my home."

"Your 'home' is in a condemned building!" I was losing control. What was wrong with her? Was she senile? Couldn't she see?

"You're not like Doyle. You're not the kind daughter he told me about. The smart girl who got good jobs and volunteered to charities, who took care of him to the end. Oh, poor Doyle."

"I'm not a girl," I whispered. I didn't want to cry, wished she wouldn't mention him.

"Really? You are to me. To your dad."

She looked up at me with the watery eyes of an old lady who'd just lost her best friend.

"Dad's gone." My voice began to break. Tears spilled onto my cheeks. "I'm the *last* one!" I didn't want to yell at her, but I did.

We stared at each other, saying nothing. Only street sounds came into her apartment—cars honking, workers laughing, a pipe striking the sidewalk. She lifted her hand to reach out to me, then stopped and pulled back.

"Then I guess we're stuck with each other."

She looked down at the skirt of her housecoat, threadbare at her knees, then put her hands in the pockets.

"What clothes do you want me to pack?"

She didn't answer.

"What do you want me to pack?" I repeated, and went to pick up the large suitcase that I'd brought.

"Not a damn thing!" a deep, steady voice behind me boomed.

I dropped the suitcase, turned, and saw a tall, bald man in shirt and tie stooped in the shadow of the bedroom door. He leaned on a wooden cane with a carved monkey head for a handle. He held an empty bucket in his left hand. I saw water dripping from the ceiling in the bedroom behind him.

CHAPTER 2

COUSIN ELLA WALKED toward the man and rested her hand on his.

Her face tightened. "Jack, I got this. I told her we're staying." I heard a strength in her voice, a finality that I'd have to fight.

Just then, behind them, water from the bedroom ceiling began gushing down. They slowly turned around to see it, so I lunged toward Jack, snatched his bucket, and ran through the door. The leak was above the unmade bed. I started to clear a path between mounds of housedresses, dingy white shirts, other dirty laundry, and piles of junk.

Jack yelled after me. "That's my job! You got no right going in there."

I ignored him and pushed ahead. Cousin Ella and Jack tried to follow me, but they—especially Jack with his cane—weren't fast enough. If valuables were in there, I didn't want them ruined.

My jeans got wet as I positioned the bucket on the bed under peeling paint and the cracks in the ceiling where the water rained in from the roof. I heard Cousin Ella in the kitchen banging pots. Then she hobbled into the room on the path I'd made to bring me two rusty casserole pans. Cousin Ella came over to the bed. She touched the bed linens and mattress where they were soaked. We had nothing to say. She left the bedroom, shaking her head and mumbling something about sleeping. By now the stream of water had subsided to a few drips.

She sat beside Jack on the sofa in the living room. He put his arm around her shoulders and she rested her head on his chest.

"C'mon, Carrie, relax and come out of there," she said, but I didn't follow her. If they weren't going to help themselves, I had to do it. I had no time for aged lovebirds.

Rumpled clothes, old show posters in French, empty whiskey and Pinot Noir bottles, and whatever else were in piles around the bedroom. Some stacks were as high as my waist. The tallest mound was under the window right in front of me, and I went for that.

I threw the black and brown fedoras with droopy brims and five torn skirts—balled up, probably for mending years ago—into the small space in the corner. I threw disgusting stained undies—men's and women's—there, too. Underneath the pile of clothes I felt something tall, hard, and boxlike. I swept my arm across the top of it to see what it was.

The screen of the old Admiral TV and hi-fi combo that used to be in my family's living room stared me in the face. I bent down to get a better look. The TV screen was encrusted with sticky dust. Yes, this was it. This was Dad's favorite possession. He'd stored his Duke Ellington, Sarah Vaughan, Count Basie, Billie Holiday, and all his other jazz albums in the lower cabinet. On his time off from his night shift, his modest joy was listening to them while sipping a Scotch and soda. He'd say "hi-fi" with pride because, to him, hi-fi was the latest thing—and he had been able to buy it.

When he had time off his shift, he also enjoyed every *Playhouse 90* play, Uncle Miltie's comedy, *Early Show* movie, and news show that he could find in *TV Guide*. I could remember only once when he was annoyed by what was on that TV. It was when Langston was on a show. Dad was a subway conductor then. This was on a night before he started visiting Cousin Ella. After dinner, he sat quietly on the sofa in the dark before he turned on the TV. Mom was alive then, too. Even as she cleaned the kitchen, she was beautiful with her two black braids pinned across the top of her head like a crown. Any other night when he was off from work, she'd have plopped down on the sofa beside Dad to watch their shows together. But she was taking longer than usual with her chores.

He didn't wait for her and turned on the TV. But little girl me? Yes, of course, I'd watch anything on the new TV anytime. That night I saw a show I'd never heard of. Black-and-white fuzzy images with a pleasant man named Langston Hughes and some guy he called Semple.

Mom popped her head in the living room. "What's that you're watching?"

When Dad didn't respond, she slunk back into the kitchen. He just sat there staring at the moving images on the screen as if he'd somehow projected himself into it, as if he were sitting there with Langston and his friends. He didn't notice me, didn't ask me about my homework. His breathing was heavy, faster than normal. I'd felt my hands go cold as he sat there taking longer sips of his drink. I was trying to watch the show, but I felt strange. Dad didn't laugh when Semple said something funny. Dad just sat. Silent.

I got fidgety and wiggled on the floor closer to the TV. I inspected Langston's face. Something was familiar to me about him. The more I watched him, the more I saw my dad's eyes, mine, too. The face shape and color were the same. Langston was older, but I couldn't doubt his resemblance to Dad. I wanted to ask Dad about him, but Dad's stone face made me afraid to ask.

By the time the show was over, I'd had no idea what this man on TV meant to Dad—if he meant anything at all. I was confused about Dad's reaction to a funny TV show. Mom stayed in the kitchen doing crosswords. Dad picked up his empty glass and refilled it from the bottle next to his feet. He got up, turned off the TV, and took an album from the cabinet. He put Billie Holiday's "God Bless the Child" on the turntable.

I went to bed but couldn't sleep. He was still playing it when Mom quietly slipped off to bed alone. He played it all night.

"You thought that TV was long gone, didn't you?"

I turned to see that Cousin Ella had been watching me through the door.

"Is this my gift?" I asked.

"What gift?" She had a sly, I-know-something-you-don't look. It was a little smirk that lifted her scarred cheek.

"Dad told me that you have something for me."

"Oh, that! Yeah, baby, you gotta earn that. But you can have that old TV. Hasn't worked in years. Maybe you can do something with it."

"Are you playing me?"

A crease deepened between her eyes. "No." She looked toward the TV. "Y'know, they had a hard time getting that up here."

OK, I'd play along. "Who?"

"Langston and Doyle, of course."

"Really? Dad and Langston were here together?"

"Well, you know your Dad was always up on new things. He just had to have a new Sylvania TV with something called 'halolight,' I think. So he offered me this old one. We only wanted it for the hi-fi record player. Anyway, one July morning after his night working the subway, he came by sweaty and tired. I don't know where he found someone with a truck to bring it to the sidewalk out there but he was stuck with it at the building's door. He yelled up at our windows and good thing Langston was here. He was a shorter fella than Doyle. A little skinnier, too. He didn't have your mom's cooking to broaden him out."

She didn't know that Mom didn't cook much. It was Dad who loved to create in the kitchen. Mom just cleaned up.

She was staring toward the window and went on.

"That day Langston was dressed so neat in a shirt and tie, but he helped, and they managed to get that TV into the elevator and in here. We used to have it in the living room. It was fine for playing music when we had salons and Langston wanted to dance. When it broke down, we dragged it in here the best we could. Couldn't move it anywhere else."

As Dad would have done it, I opened the cabinet to see the record player on the unit. I touched the turntable as if it were fragile china. My chest started to heave, and I slammed the unit shut. I felt Cousin Ella's stares, saw dust fly everywhere, and smelled wet plaster on the ceiling and old booze bottles.

"You're taking his passing hard, aren't you? We all miss him, but you're the daughter. That's gotta be different."

Was she trying to make me cry again? I tried not to hear her. I looked around the room. I had to start sifting through all that clutter.

"I'll tell you why he left his conductor job. At least, why he said—"

My phone rang. When I answered, I was grateful for Bill's call; it forced Ella, with her old-school etiquette, to leave the bedroom.

"No, I haven't started yet. There's a lot—would you let me finish? I said . . . yes, I know you have to start your job . . . the lawyer said what? . . . This afternoon? . . . OK, OK. I'll be there . . . love you."

As usual, he was impatient with me. The connection had already gone quiet, as if he'd put his thumb on the phone to end the call before he'd heard me.

I saw Cousin Ella's head pop around the doorframe. Her etiquette aside, I knew she'd been listening.

"As I was saying, you remember around that time he gave that TV to us, he started working in the post office?"

"I guess so. But, look, I have to get boxes to pack your stuff." I couldn't let this old woman's stories slow me down and make me late to the lawyer's appointment. I didn't want to lose the condo sale. Yet, I felt drawn in to what she was saying about Dad.

"Listen. I think your dad was ashamed of himself. I didn't know why, but early on Doyle told me he didn't like coming here when I had those salons. That changed. Yeah, those were some good times—artists, dancers, writers loved it here."

She caught herself drifting and looked directly at me.

"It was bad enough that he saw all that drinking, dancing, and good conversation when he had to go to work in the subway. I told him, he should be glad that he had a good job. But he really had problems coming around here with my groceries when Langston was here. I didn't understand that. Langston wasn't bothering anyone. He had his own problems. You know,

I never really understood how Doyle—or Langston either—had money and time for me."

"Yes, I know Dad brought you groceries. He said you didn't have enough money . . ."

She was pulling me in. I wanted to hear more about Dad.

"Well, that was partly wrong. It was after the war. Jack had come back from Paris by then. He'd brought enough with him to help me get small necessities, and Langston paid my rent. Sometimes, if an artist who enjoyed my salon sold a painting, they'd pitch in a little toward booze. But I think all that irked Doyle. Why? I guess his charity was more complicated than I'd thought."

I wanted to know more about her salons, but instead I scanned the room. I needed a system for sorting junk. My eye kept stopping at Cousin Ella's red, fringed dance dress on the floor behind her feet. It was the same dress that I saw in the photo in Dad's box. When I walked toward it for a closer look, she frowned and walked backward, mule-kicking the dress under another nearby pile.

I felt compelled to reminisce.

"I saw Dad once on a train when he was working overtime. He looked awkward and tired in that dark blue uniform—like it didn't fit him right in the shoulders. He quickly smiled at me, then watched the passengers. At home, he told me that he felt responsible for the passengers' safety. He used to tell me stories of people on the train. Lost kids, drunks, men mashing women, crazy people ranting nonsense. Actually,

I think he made up a lot of those stories, just to make the job interesting."

Cousin Ella was quiet, fidgeting in her pocket. She said, "I bet he didn't tell you this one. Doyle said that one morning when he was finishing his night shift on, you know, that train that comes uptown here, he saw Langston sprawled out on a seat by himself. Langston was dressed neat as he could be—white shirt and tie, tailored overcoat—and was reading a book. Some photographer was taking his picture. Doyle said that he felt trapped and suffocated in his uniform. Well, that would have been bad enough for Doyle's feelings—you know how sensitive he was—but Langston didn't take half a minute to say hello to him. Doyle always resented that."

"If it was a photo shoot, then Langston was busy. He might not have even noticed Dad."

"Yeah, I know, but that's not how Doyle took it. He said that made him feel like nothing—like he was a piece of crap in Langston's view of things."

"Was that Langston's view?"

I'd observed when I was very young that Dad was always so ready for slights. Once, I heard Mom try to compliment him on how he looked when they went out. He told her outright that she was wrong, as if he was embarrassed about making himself look good.

"I doubt it. I don't know what was in his head. But I do know that Langston was friendly. He could talk to everyone. Yeah, he was probably distracted. All I know is that Doyle got a job in the post office so he wouldn't have to see Langston in the subway anymore."

"He told me it was to make more money."

"Yeah, that too. He knew he had to save more if you were going to go to college. But really, all I know is that things changed after that."

"Why are you telling me this about Dad and Langston?"

"Because I bet you want to know some of the history. It's important."

"Look. Right now, I'm ready to get you out of this place. We can talk later."

She smiled at me. Her housedress blended in with the piles of clutter around her. The red dress in the pile at her feet was a flash of color that I wanted to see, but she stood guard in front of it.

She said quietly but deliberately, "I want you out of this bedroom. Jack said you had no right to be in here." She stood as straight as she could and pointed a finger at the door to the living room. I hesitated. She pointed her arm with a dancer's grace that I didn't expect, and she stood there until I moved. She followed me.

CHAPTER 3

＋

WHEN I CAME OUT of the bedroom, Jack was still sitting on the sofa, holding a tumbler half-filled with whiskey. He turned and lifted the glass toward me. His hand shook. "You took liberties with our things."

"The construction workers will take more than liberties." I had no patience with niceties.

He ignored me and eased back into the sofa's cushions. I barely heard Billie Holiday singing a scratchy "God Bless the Child." It was playing softly from a small record player on the table next to him. It was just as well that he was caught up in the music and not with me. I wanted to be done with this without distraction from him, whoever he was to Cousin Ella.

I just had to deal with this the way I always focused on my projects at work. I had a strong sense of how to organize details and people. At work, I had a good, cooperative team that I was already missing. Bill didn't think I was paid enough, so he had little respect for it, but I was good at it. So, yes, if I dealt with Jack and

Cousin Ella the way I managed at work, I'd have no problem.

"Dance with me." Jack was looking in my direction with droopy eyes.

"What? I have to—"

"No, not you." He swatted the air with his empty hand as if I were a fly. He was looking past me as he put down his drink.

I turned around and Cousin Ella was walking from the doorway toward him with a little bounce in her steps. She smiled as she took his hand to help him from the sofa. He leaned on her, as he would on his cane. Cousin Ella closed her eyes. Jack balanced himself enough to gently touch the scar on her cheek. His eyes glistened. I thought he would cry, but he didn't. I felt Lady Day's music. I caught myself swaying to the slow beat. I wanted to dance, too.

I needed to move, to get back to work. I tiptoed past them to pick up the suitcase that I'd left next to the sofa. Cousin Ella was still dancing when she opened her eyes and watched me take the bag into the bedroom. When I closed the door within a few inches, there wasn't much light. I had to see better so I opened the blinds with a fragile, half-rotted cord. All the slats were grimy and brown from many hot summers of being open to car exhaust rising from the street. A few slats were bent and broken. The slant rays of daylight were bright enough for me to see the wearable clothes I'd sorted near the TV. I needed to choose from that pile the wardrobe that would be most useful to Cousin Ella.

The frayed nightgowns and panties with loose elastic had to be laundered, but we didn't have time for that. I tossed them in the suitcase. I had no idea what to do with Jack's clothes. Actually, I had no idea what to do with Jack. Cousin Ella and he seemed inseparable. They were still dancing. I wasn't looking forward to taking her away from him. Maybe if they were married I'd have a chance at getting him into the assisted-living apartment with her, but I doubted they'd bothered.

I started another pile for Jack's clothes. His clothes were higher quality than Cousin Ella's. Some of his wide-collared, double-breasted jackets had traces of hand-stitching. The seams were torn in some of them, but I knew they must have been custom-made. Goodness knows what he might have done to get them, but he had to have been wealthier decades ago. I imagined him in the crushed fedoras and rumpled blue pinstriped suits that I was piling next to the open bag with Cousin Ella's things. He must have been a dapper dude. No wonder Cousin Ella fell for him.

The bittersweet music of "God Bless the Child" in the living room had stopped. I could hear Cousin Ella's footsteps coming toward the bedroom door. Her old red dress was just an arm's length from me. Close up I could see ripped threads with missing sequins. It had a few small holes as if moths had gotten to it. Its lipstick red had faded to brown along a few crease lines. So, this was the hootchy-kootchy dress that Mom, a preacher's daughter, so despised.

I thought I saw a doll's legs in a clear plastic bag sticking out from under the side of the dress. I wanted to see it better, but Cousin Ella had positioned herself in front of the dress again. Over her flower-embroidered slippers, her ankles looked swollen, puffy. Did she have a heart problem?

"Why are you so nosy?"

It felt like she was a hawk, ready to swoop down on me if I made the wrong move. For the moment, I didn't know what to do. She was looking at my sorted piles.

"These aren't my best clothes. You know that, right?"

"OK. Where are they?" I scanned the clutter around the room.

"In Paris. Where I left them when the war started to get bad."

That was just when Dad was arriving. I didn't want to think about it. "OK. I'm not going there to pack."

"I did. I went there—to *Paree*—when I left the Cotton Club. I was tired of dancing in that segregated club. Can you imagine? Whites only in Harlem. I figured if I had to do that, I might as well see the world doing it. But most of all, I wanted to make a name for myself. Me. Not some anonymous dancer like I was on the chorus line. So one of the girls told me about Bricktop in Paris."

"What's that?"

"You don't know? Carrie, my dear, Bricktop was a black ex-patriate. More motivated than anyone I could think of at that time. Anyway, she owned clubs and, as luck would have it, I met her at one of her parties. When I got to talk to her, I told her I was a dancer. She let me try out. I guess I was good enough for her to give me a job."

She was looking off in space, toward the open blinds, as she spoke.

"I was excited at first. But when I got to the club for rehearsal, I was in the chorus line again. Except for people talking French, it was as if I'd stayed in Harlem."

Light moved in streaks across her scar. She didn't notice that I was back to packing her dirty undies. Some were black and silky, others had frills and lace. All had frayed elastic waists. Some were so stretched they had safety pins to keep them from slipping past her hips. I heard the sounds of construction men loading a dump truck in the street. I had to pack faster.

"I guess I was doing well enough. Got my name on the program a few times. Some of the gentlemen patrons said they liked the way I shook that fringe. They liked my moves, my energy. They said I was pretty. Some, usually the very drunk ones, wanted to touch, but I didn't let them—at least not as much as they wanted. When that caused trouble, sometimes, if they weren't spending enough, they were thrown out. I couldn't stand their whiskey breath, but when I started up with Jack I got used to it. You know, I really just wanted to dance, dance my heart out."

"So Jack was the man in the photo."

"Of course."

Just then, I noticed a small filigree jewelry box. Its gold finish glistened under a web of wrinkled ties. I held my breath. Given the quality of some paintings and artifacts in the living room, I suspected she must have valuable jewelry too. I had my hopes that whatever it might be, Cousin Ella would let me sell it. Yes, I had savings. But since the funds from the condo sale would go straight to the new house, it would help to have more money of my own to maintain me while I tried to find just the right job. But when I picked up the box, the bottom fell off. The hinges on the lid were broken too. Cousin Ella saw the long strands of cheap pearls, feathered earrings, and dried roses falling out. My brief hope of extra cash ended.

"Now look what you've done!"

I let her see me pick up the trinkets, tie them in a kerchief, and place the bundle on the dresser before Cousin Ella could bend down to put them back in the broken box. I didn't want her to think that I would put her precious junk on the mounding trash pile.

"I wore those pearls every night when I danced. Did you see how all those necklaces are different styles? I had one for every outfit. But in my heyday, mostly, I wore this red dress. Since the men seemed to like that, it got them to spend more at the club. Bricktop liked that."

When she pointed to the dress, rumpled as it was, I wanted to see her in it.

"Why don't you hold it up to your shoulders to show me how it looked in the photo you sent Dad?"

She shook her head.

"That photo . . . there's too much bad in that dress. That was the last time I took it off. I swore I'd never wear it again."

With that, I didn't dare move to touch the dress or the subject.

"I knew I could dance better than Baker. Bricktop told me so. But Josephine showed her titties all over the place. I think Bricktop liked that. But you wouldn't catch me doing that. No, no! So I never got to be the star. I kept my principles!"

I had been quietly sorting the pile of undies and was almost finished packing them when I tried to imagine Cousin Ella wearing a banana skirt à la Baker. I looked up at her in her housedress with her hands on her hips, head up. She was proud of herself, yes, but it was probably her modesty—feigned or not—that kept her from top billing, though she was very beautiful in that old photo that she had sent to Dad to show him how well she was doing in Paris. Now I wondered if she really had done as well as she wanted him to believe. How devastating would it be for her to have gone all the way to Paris only to fail at her dream. She was a proud, shapely dancer in that red dress, with manicured nails and old-style perfect makeup with pencil lines for eyebrows. She highlighted her lovely full lips with dark lipstick. Her eyes were naturally expressive—but that scar . . . what happened to her? She kept talking, so I didn't bring it up.

"After all, Bricktop was good to me. She kept me on as a dancer, which is what I wanted more than anything, until, until this!"

When she pointed to the scar a crease appeared between her eyes. She didn't notice that I had closed the suitcase that I'd stuffed with her clothes.

When I stood I saw she was breathing deeply. I wanted to check her to make sure she was OK. But she turned the scarred cheek away from me and closed her eyes.

"That's where I saw Langston, you know. He was young, really sweet looking. Yeah, we all were young then. He was a cook over there in Montmartre at some other club. Whenever I saw him, he was writing his poems on some scrap of paper. He looked familiar. One day, I got curious about him. When we started talking about people we were related to, we knew we were cousins. But he'd grown up in the Midwest and I—like your dad—was raised here in Harlem. But in Paris just being there for each other made us feel like home. Every time one of us would feel down, we'd meet for a drink. I had a little more money than he did, so I could help him out when he needed it. I was like his big sister."

I went for a pile of shoes to start sorting.

"Y'know, Langston could talk some French. I couldn't. He helped me understand what was going on."

"How long were you in Paris?"

She turned away. "Not long. Not long enough."

Some of the black satin pumps had broken heels. Rhinestone bows had chipped off other pairs and had dropped below into the arches of the black and brown men's shoes. The dried-out leather was cracked and the fibers in the shoe strings were stripped apart. The soles were worn out.

"We used to dance in those shoes, me and Jack. We were like one person when we danced. We were always so in sync."

Her dancing shoes were like mine, those that I'd bagged and put in the dumpster the day before. They were the last items I culled from my closet. I couldn't justify packing them to move cross country. I felt sadness that I'd have to toss out Cousin Ella's dancing shoes, too. She hadn't worn them for decades and never would again, but as soon as I threw them on the junk pile, I felt compelled to reach for them, to take them back. I resisted. My practical side knew that there was no reason to keep unwearable shoes.

She was staring at those shoes, then smiled.

"Do you know what it's like to love like that, Carrie? When your heart beats to the same rhythm as another person's? I felt like that with Jack, until there was a time I didn't. But, well, I do feel that now. And you, Carrie, what do you feel?"

I looked for more shoes to sort. I could think of nothing to say.

"Doyle, your father had his steady paycheck, y'know. Back then Doyle thought that because Langston's books were everywhere, he must have been rich since he was famous. But for as long as I knew him, Langston always had to scrape by. Your dad found that out later—about how poor some of us artists were when you were in college. Some of us lived on the whims of patrons. Others worked when they could.

That's why he wanted you to be secure in a good job and marriage. Back then he'd say that fame didn't pay anyone's rent. As for me, not that I was famous, I knew that too well. Bricktop paid me just enough to get a room with two other girls she'd hired. Hah! We always thought she knew that walking up those stairs would sure keep our legs strong for dancing. Yeah, I was young, but those stairs wore me out."

She opened her eyes and stared at me. She didn't move. I sat on the dry edge of the chenille bedspread and focused on the sticky, cleared space on the hardwood floor where the shoes had been. Outside, a construction worker was yelling something in Spanglish. Horns, loud in the street, echoed on the wet ceiling. There was a staccato rhythm to the street noise. When I looked up, Cousin Ella was watching me.

"Why don't you talk to me, Carrie? What are you holding in?"

I bit my lip hard. I licked my warm blood.

"I came here to get you to a safe place. We'll have time to talk when that's done."

"Really? You know I just heard you on the phone talking, I think, with your husband, with Bill."

"Yeah, so? He wanted to know how I was doing, what progress I was making."

"Is that why you're so flustered? Or is that none of my business?"

"We're moving to Seattle tomorrow. I have lots of my own stuff to do this afternoon."

"Langston passed through there. He said Seattle was OK—a bunch of mountains and trees. What's there for you?"

"A good job."

"I thought you had one here."

I saw colorful hat boxes stacked in the corner. I got up to tackle those next. I felt her eyes piercing my back.

"Carrie, you move like a dancer. You haven't lost it. I bet you know that."

Cousin Ella sat silently on the bed.

I was grateful. I didn't want to hear any more of her jabber. I had too much work to do. But packing up Cousin Ella's life—and my own—wasn't the work I wanted. I should have been at my desk in the office. I knew I couldn't go back. I'd already trained Alice to take over my job. She was good. But me? I had copies of my new résumé and a list of references in a folder in my tote bag—ready to take on the plane tomorrow night.

Bill said he was looking out for me and I was thankful for his help. He'd set up a few interviews for me with business friends of his. I didn't know any of them. I think they were in his fraternity network. The jobs they offered me were so-so managerial. But, I guessed, it would be a way to start in a new city. I'd have to get used to that new home. Anyway, Bill would have a good engineering job to pay our mortgage. I could take my time job searching, maybe even have time to learn to cook a good pot of greens, like Dad did.

"Carrie, if you won't talk to me, I want to tell you this."

This woman couldn't shut up.

"I think it was about twenty years ago when Doyle came here to bring his usual delivery of groceries. That man was so good to me, rest his soul! He was acting kind of nervous when he stored the produce in the icebox, no, I mean, the refrigerator. When he closed the fridge door, I saw his cheeks were wet. Your father was crying. He told me he knew he'd hurt you."

"What?" Her words were rubbing the raw grief I'd held in since Dad had passed.

She paused. I could think of many small slights my adolescent mind had resented back then. Usually they were about the chores that Mom used to do that I inherited—laundry, vacuuming. One day he heard me mumble, "I'm not your maid." He raised his hand to slap me, then turned away. I didn't say that again. I knew we both missed Mom. Dad and I should have talked about that. We never did.

I looked up at Cousin Ella.

"He told me about some audition you went to."

"Oh, that . . ."

She watched me fumble with Jack's straw hats. I put them down on the bed and kneeled on the floor to pull another pile from under the bed. Her face tightened. She stood and kicked the red dress further away from me, as if she hated it, and turned toward the living room.

"What did he tell you?" I whispered.

"He said it was when you were in college. That you

almost blew your chances with Bill. Doyle was proud of you that you got Bill to marry you, I know. He wanted you to be happy. He'd just found out about his heart problems. He had no idea that he'd live as long as he did. He wanted you to be settled."

"Settled? Why did he tell you this?"

She heard me, but looked away.

"He said he was proud of you and ashamed of himself for trying to force you, 'a square peg in a round hole.' Ha! He talked like a woodworker sometimes."

"But why did he tell you that? He could have told me that himself."

I wasn't sure of what I was feeling. I knew that this was not what I wanted to think about. It made me hate Dad at a time when I loved and missed him so much.

"He had his own problems. Your mother was dead. She was no friend of mine, but I did feel bad about the accident. Poor woman. That car messed up her body pretty bad. Your dad was in shock. He had to do double duty then, working the night shift in the post office to hold the two of you together and trying to put you through college. He had to keep his strength up when you were too young in the head to notice how tired he was."

Jack hobbled toward the bedroom door. He saw me holding a fedora.

"Ella, come on outta there, and get that girl out, too. I don't want her foolin' with my things."

"Soon, Jack, soon."

Cousin Ella had scratched a wound. I think she knew that I needed a moment to heal.

CHAPTER 4

✦

WHEN I WAS READY to get out of my own head, I saw Cousin Ella whispering to Jack in the living room. I went to confront her, but when she saw me, she came to me.

"I'd heard that a great dancer, Tyree Jones, was holding auditions in Harlem for his new fusion dance group," I said. Talking about this made me queasy.

Cousin Ella sat on the dry side of the bed, listening intently. "He'd been the lead in a group in San Francisco, right?"

She patted the space next to her for me to sit. When I did, I sank into a soft spot in the mattress. I shifted to get my balance.

"Yes. Once, the previous year, I saw him dance at Lincoln Center. I stared at him the whole time. I felt I was in the moment with him. What he could do with his tall, strong body—his grace!"

As I spoke of his dance, my legs moved slightly on their own, as if I were his partner. Cousin Ella saw that and smiled. I forced myself to stop moving.

I thought of this memory that I'd pushed back for years. Until yesterday, I had been content to layer it over with the work of balance sheets, marketing plans, and talk of human resources. Why did I feel this was the time to spill this out, in her cluttered, condemned bedroom?

Cousin Ella said, "But he'd just had a falling out with the director of that group. Tyree had studied and practiced everything—modern, ballet, jazz, even folk of many cultures. He was a dance genius, but he didn't think he was respected enough in San Francisco."

She knew Tyree Jones by his first name?

I said, "There was the rumor that he wanted to start his own group in New York. Then I read that it was true, in a newspaper that Dad left on the kitchen table. He always left it for me when he was done with it. When Dad was at work during the day, I practiced in the living room to his jazz albums. I did my own choreography. That was OK, but the audition motivated me to take dance more seriously. This was my chance! A longshot, yes. But I felt compelled to try out."

"I would've felt the same way."

"But you did do the same thing. You were really a dancer."

She was quiet, looking down at her hands. "For a while."

"Cousin Ella, just as you said, I knew Dad had high

hopes for me, but I was barely getting through my accounting class. Not because I couldn't do it. It was just that I didn't care. I knew dancing was a risk—that I might lose my scholarship if I used my time practicing my routine in that dance class at the Y—the best that I could afford—instead of reviewing for final exams. But I needed this."

"I know that need. First time I had it was when I tried out for the Cotton Club. My mother, like yours, was a good sister in the church. God rest her soul . . . she didn't want me shakin' my butt in front of all those white patrons, but I had to dance. The Cotton Club was the best place in the city for me."

When they tore down the Savoy in the late fifties to build those high-rise apartments across the street, I'd wondered what had happened to the dreams of young women like Cousin Ella. But me, I was more modern. I had had my sights on dancing with Tyree Jones.

"Then you know why I needed to push myself and do better than the others in that class. I did that easily. And I wished I could pay for more professional classes. I needed the challenge. But I had little money left after buying textbooks. My cashier job at Macy's—and what I'd saved from skipping lunch—was just enough to pay for the class at the Y. I practiced at home alone every minute I could."

"What did Doyle think of those classes?"

"I didn't tell Dad what I was doing. You know I couldn't. There was one morning, as I was leaving for class he was just getting home from work. I knew he'd been drinking with his friends because he slurred his words when he asked me, 'What've you got in that backpack? Books aren't round and soft like that.' I didn't answer him. He pushed on. 'It looks like a change of clothes to me, especially since I can see that black cloth poking out of the zipper.' He didn't bother me about it then. But I knew I had to do better at hiding my dance clothes between the fat business books."

"So, Carrie, you lied to him. You didn't tell him what you were doing, so you lied."

"I hadn't thought of it as a lie. I thought of it as my soul's survival." Why was she taking his side?

She got fidgety, then got up slowly and left the room. She came back into the room to sit on the bed next to me. She looked like a stern, old-style schoolmarm.

My throat got tense. I didn't want to be so close to her. Yes, I'd felt guilty when I snuck out of the apartment that day when I was on my way to dance class, but I didn't want to hear her accusations. I didn't need that from her. She was a dancer herself, after all. She should have understood. Anyway, now I was being loyal to Dad by helping her. I stood and faced her.

She said, "You know you didn't have to lie. Doyle was a softy. If you had told him that, you know that he would've given in, eventually."

Maybe she was right. Could be that I didn't feel truly confident enough to dance professionally back then. Did Dad know that? I persisted with Cousin Ella.

"You can call it a lie if you want, but I couldn't wait that long. I had to go to dance class. This was my last one before the audition. For that hour and a half, I forgot about the C that I got on both my statistics midterm and the late paper for my management class. The only time that existed for me was the music's drumbeat. When I danced, I forgot Mom's death, the way Bill ignored me on campus, Dad's drinking and moodiness. It was just me in that moment when it was stuffy and humid in that studio. I flowed through it, sweaty, sure, but I remember now that I danced so hard that, for the first time in my life, I pulled a tendon in my calf. This was the day before the audition! I think my stress caused me to work too hard."

She turned her face away from me. I wondered if her scar went deeper than the surface of her skin.

"When I nearly limped in the apartment door after that class, my clothes were damp and stinky. Dad was setting the kitchen table. It was his night off—the one night a week we had a ritual dinner together. Thank goodness that he had fixed a salad that filled the large bowls on our placemats and not his signature authentic spaghetti that he'd learned to make from his Italian coworkers. I would not have been able to handle the pasta bloat. I went into my room to put down my things and quickly taped up my calf."

Cousin Ella smiled and turned back to me. "He liked to cook, I know. He made that spaghetti here once or twice. And he didn't just plop it down on the plates. He used to make food, the place settings, too, look like a still life. Sometimes it looked too pretty to eat. He'd present our dishes to us with care, as if they were fragile masterpieces. Since Jack and I never got to restaurants, we were grateful for this. Did he cook that way for you?"

"No, especially not that night. I felt nervous when I sat across from him. I was trying to act normally, like I would any other night—talking about LBJ's Great Society, Vietnam. He liked to talk about current events. But I was pouring dressing on my salad when he pushed an envelope to the middle of the table. It was a letter from City College. He said to me, 'Read it. Open it and read it.' I put down the dressing bottle and stared at him."

I didn't want to go on, but Cousin Ella was sitting there, quietly, patiently waiting for me to continue. My anxiety of twenty years ago was rising in my throat. I became aware of sounds of clinking glass in the living room. Jack must have been getting another drink.

"Yes, and so what did you do?"

"I didn't move, but he yelled at me. 'Open it. I work hard so you can have what I couldn't. I have the right to know what's going on.'

"I thought he was only half right. Sure, he worked hard, but the letter was addressed to me. He kept glaring at me. I gave in and opened the letter. I was being warned about my grades. I felt my eyes flutter. He noticed and yelled at me again. 'I knew it wasn't good! Look. I've been watching you come home late, all sweaty. You've been hanging out with Bill, haven't you?'

"I tried to protest, but he wouldn't stop. He ranted about how Bill would lose respect for me, how hard he worked, how Mom had tried to guide me on the right path, and on and on. He said he didn't want to know what I'd been doing though he tried to guess. He liked Bill but he wanted me to stay away from him until finals were over. He drilled into me that I had to know my priorities.

"I was confused because I hadn't seen Bill in months. I liked him enough, but he was a devoted engineering major who wanted to go to grad school. He was highly motivated about this, so he lost interest in seeing me when I told him I was skipping accounting to go to dance class. Funny that, a few months later when I stopped being 'foolish,' as he called it, about dancing, he asked me out again. He liked my dancer's body. We said we were in love, but at that age it was probably in lust."

I paused. Cousin Ella patted my arm. That encouraged me to go on. This was all so incredibly vivid to me after years of holding it in. Letting it out felt good.

"At that point, I sensed it was best to let Dad believe his theory about Bill and me. I told him I understood what he'd said. I think I mumbled, 'I'm sorry.' He smiled at that. He seemed sure that he'd succeeded in getting me back on track."

"So, did you ever get to see Tyree?"

"Well, the next morning, Dad slept late. This was usually what he did when he'd had the previous night off—and a few drinks while listening to Ahmad Jamal. So that morning, he didn't see me sneaking out with my backpack bulging with change of dancewear. I was determined to go to the audition. It was in a church basement about ten blocks away. I walked to clear my head. My calf didn't hurt as much as I'd expected, though I could feel remnants of pain when I stepped on that leg."

Cousin Ella was getting animated. "Tyree Jones looked even taller close up, didn't he? Yeah. His body had the precision and poise of the master dancer he was." She was beaming.

"Yes, he did. There were about ten of us there to audition. The other dancers looked focused and ready, like they'd done this before. This was my first audition. I was such an amateur! Honestly, I didn't even notice it when it was my turn. Tyree yelled at me twice. Then I just knew I wanted to dance, so I moved. I loved the way my whole body became one with the music. I danced the routine through my pain. I didn't feel it in my calf. I guess it was mind over matter. I had worked hard for this. I felt my life depended on this dance."

Cousin Ella was staring at every feature of my face. That felt creepy, but I couldn't stop talking.

"After the last dancer had finished, Tyree told us to line up against the back wall of the church basement. I'd heard this was the only place Tyree Jones could afford to hold these auditions. He pointed at me with his strong, sinewy fingers. I looked at the girls to my left and right. I thought he meant one of them, but they were looking at me. The tan girl to my left was crying.

"'Carrie Stevens, come up here!' When Tyree called out my name my knees buckled, but I caught myself on the barre. I knew I had my chance.

"He looked impatient. 'Yes, it's you.' And just like that Tyree Jones took me on for the lead. He pointed to a few others to fill out the troupe."

Cousin Ella giggled like a sixteen-year-old. I paused. That sound from a ninety-something's scarred face was unnerving. She was gleeful.

"And?"

"He told us to stay. He performed a segment of the dance we were to learn. At first, I was simply entranced by his ease of movement. Then, when he did it again, he expected us to know it. I did it perfectly.

"When I left, my leg was throbbing, so I took the bus home to our apartment. But I ran in the door, almost into Dad, who had just finished coffee before leaving for his night shift. I saw that he'd been in my room. At that point, I didn't care. Some of my dance-wear and the flyer announcing today's audition were on the kitchen table. My heart was racing too fast to quibble about the invasion of my privacy. I picked up the announcement and shook it at him. I almost screamed.

'I danced out of my skin. I got it, Dad, I got it!'"

Cousin Ella held my hands. I felt she knew what came next.

"I will always remember what he said then."

After years of suppressing his words, I was having trouble getting them out. I was shaking.

"It's OK. You can talk to me. I don't gossip. There's no one for me to tell this to. Almost everyone I knew is gone. You can trust me."

I'd never spoken of this. I was surprised that I could confide in her. But this old woman would have no one to repeat my story to. She might even forget everything I said. There would be no rumors about it from her. I had run this audition through my mind for years. It was a cycle. It would fester and blast its way into my mind. Then I would squash it by throwing myself into overwhelming work projects, a long and tedious to-do list of chores, chocolate cake, facials—anything to make the memory disappear and for me to regain some sense of balance. But now, I felt compelled to get it out and over with.

"He said, 'That's nice.' Then he just walked out to go to work and shut the door.

"I cried all night. In the morning, I did my best to pull myself together and I called Tyree. When I told him I couldn't be in his troupe, he asked, 'Are you sure?' I whispered, 'Yes.' He said, 'OK, good luck,' and hung up. That was it."

I was exhausted from telling this to Cousin Ella. Neither of us spoke for a few minutes. Finally, when I looked at her, I was shocked. She had the biggest smile I'd seen all morning. How could another dancer, even an old one like her, respond like that?

"Your father told us how sorry he was about that, but he wanted you to be able to support yourself and be a good helpmate for Bill."

52

"A helpmate? And who were 'us'?"

"Doyle was here one night when only a few friends had come by for one of my salons. He'd already had a few drinks when Langston popped in late. Doyle really did feel bad but he didn't want . . ."

"Didn't want what?" I felt my temper rising.

"He didn't want you to wind up like me. Poor, out of work, depending on relatives and salons with a donation bucket."

I couldn't feel sorry for her. I thought she'd lived the life she wanted. As far as I was concerned, she chose that. But how did it go for me? After Mom died, Dad couldn't make up for her, but he tried. He showed me how to cook and clean. He had a job. I felt all along, by his own actions, that he was molding me into his ideal woman—a productive helpmate for her husband. My being a dancer didn't fit his view.

"So, he thought he could decide that for me!"

"Look, Langston tried to get Doyle to see that he was living OK on his writing. Sure, some months it might have been slim pickin's for his bank account, but Langston usually could find a way to eat and pay his rent."

"Why didn't Dad listen to him?"

"Doyle listened to him. But when he was done, Doyle just looked at Langston and then stared at me. His face may as well have been granite. That's all he needed to do to make his point. He made me feel bad, like a charity case, in front of my guests."

"Who else knew about me?"

"Anyone who'd listen. Doyle loved talking about you, how smart you were, and what a great future you'd have."

I asked myself if this was the future he imagined I'd have.

"Let's go!" Cousin Ella was shooing me out of the room. I lagged behind her.

For years, I had held in this anger. For a second, I wished Dad hadn't died so I could confront him on this pain he caused. I would tell him how hard I had worked for that audition. But having released some of my pain, I wondered if I was being fair to him. I remembered that he could've sent me to live with his mother. Some of his friends suggested that. But he chose to be a loyal father. I took a few long breaths to calm myself. At that moment, it occurred to me that I might have caused my own pain. I could have chosen not to call Tyree.

But how could I really complain? If I'd been a dancer, I probably wouldn't have had the salary I needed to buy my condo. I knew I surely wouldn't have married Bill. He had no interest in dancing. He wouldn't even dance with me at his brother's wedding, and danced only once—I'm sure because he felt it was an obligation—at our own. When others were dancing, I spent a lot of my time sitting at the wedding party table, talking to my bridesmaid about how to fix the stuck zipper on her gown while his relatives came by to say their hellos and good wishes. Then they danced and laughed. But Bill was not like them. He was off talking about job prospects to another engineer at a table in the back of the hall. I was tempted to eat more wedding cake just to pass the time, but I didn't. Back then, I liked my toned body too much to gorge myself with cake. I knew over the years my attitude about that had changed—because of the rising numbers I saw on the scale. But like Dad said, Bill had been a good provider and I was lucky for that.

"C'mon, Carrie. Don't you have work to do out here?"

She was encouraging me to pack? Was she beginning to deal with the reality, the plain fact that she had to move? I hadn't finished sorting all those mounds of jumbled clothes in the bedroom.

Despite my concerns, I followed Cousin Ella back into the living room. After all, it was her apartment, not mine. Jack was still slouched on the sofa with a drink, probably his second. He opened his eyes wide when she approached him.

I heard her tell him, "I think she's OK. She'll earn it."

CHAPTER 5

✦

THE BANGING ON THE DOOR put every nerve in my body on high alert. I'd thought the construction guys would get to Cousin Ella's floor tomorrow. Were they here already? Cousin Ella, though, behaved as if it were a social call. She straightened up her dress, patted stray hair at her temples, and slowly walked toward the door. She attached the top chain lock, lifted her chin at an attractive angle, then paused before she unlocked the bolt.

With the door ajar, a woman's frantic, southern-accented voice echoed in the hallway. "Ella-Honey, let me in! They're setting up their tools and stuff on my floor! They're gonna demolish my home. I'm gonna be homeless. Homeless! Do you get what I'm saying? It'll be you, too, the day after tomorrow."

Cousin Ella calmly tilted her head in our direction to announce, "It's just Zee."

When she opened the door, I heard the metallic clatter of tools dropping on the tile hallway floor downstairs and the banter of the construction workers. The woman at the door in the tight blue sweater and bell-bottomed jeans was the same one who had shouted at me on my way upstairs. She pushed the door open and rushed in as Cousin Ella straightened her spine and closed the door. Cousin Ella looked at Zee, skeptically, from a distance, as if her apartment had just been invaded by a curious-looking Martian.

Jack sat with the cool air of an old gentleman and sipped his drink. He glanced at Zee over the rim of his glass. Across the room, the bronze art nouveau clock on the credenza caught my attention. That, with the other antiques, might be worth thousands. I'd have to pack it carefully . . . but it was already 10:30. I had no time for this panicking woman.

"Zee, this is my young cousin, Carrie," said Cousin Ella.

Zee pointed at me. When she lifted her arm, I saw that her sweater sleeve was frayed at the seam and hung open from her elbow. It fluttered as she jabbed her fingers toward me.

"Of course, I'd know her anyplace, anytime! She's my stepdaughter, Angel's older sister. She's the one who ran away with Doyle! Ella-Honey, c'mon, you remember when that happened. It was after Doyle finished those drawings of me. I knew he loved me. But he was a rat. He didn't claim Angel as his own!"

What? That startled me, to say the least. Clearly, this woman was mad. I mean, wasn't she? Her oval brown face was ashy and contorted. Her thick eyebrows went every which way. Her gray hair was matted in spots, as if she'd given up combing it. She could have been ten years older than I was—maybe close to fifty—but she looked much older. She might have been beautiful once, like Diahann Carroll, but those days were long over for her.

"Cousin Ella?" I stuttered, clearly lost.

Zee was on a rant. "Ella-Honey just don't want you to know about your daddy. He loved me, you know! Come here. Give mama a hug!" she yelled at me.

She came toward me with open arms. She stank of mustard and stale pizza. I walked backward, fast, and bumped into the credenza.

"Carrie, don't pay her any mind. Doyle didn't give her any time—"

Zee wouldn't stop. She was on a mission and I was it.

"I was cute then. You know that, Ella-Honey. Didn't you see the way Doyle smiled at me every time he saw me?"

Then she turned to me. "Your mother had just been killed in that crash. Your daddy . . . he needed me. A woman like me. I was hot to trot."

She smiled and did a little hip shake. She looked like a grinding Medusa.

"You knew my dad?" I felt bug-eyed. I was his daughter for thirty-eight years and was beginning to think I didn't know him. I wanted to hear more. Really, though, in no way could I believe that my father would be desperate enough to do anything with a crazy woman like Zee.

Then Cousin Ella was in Zee's face. It didn't seem to matter to her that she was about a foot shorter than Zee and forty years older. She was like a disciplined but caring mother, ready to give tough love.

"Now, Zee, we've got too much to do to start this nonsense. You know yourself that Carrie is Doyle and Janie's daughter. Yeah, Doyle might have smiled at you just to be friendly, but you don't get a baby from a lifted lip. You got Angel from that nice-looking Jamaican, Percy, who lived down the street, not from Doyle."

"Percy? That man told me he was going back home to some island. He left me!" Zee began to shake.

I had never seen anyone like this. Zee stunned me. Everyone I knew was reasonably sane. Sure, Cousin Ella and Jack might have been a bit daft, but not like Zee. I wanted to move away from her as far as I could. Yet I stayed in my spot. I was curious.

When Cousin Ella touched Zee's shoulder, Zee's ranting switched off. Zee whimpered, then looked down at Cousin Ella and started sobbing. Cousin Ella led Zee to the chair opposite Jack, who sat on the sofa pretending to read a dog-eared *Daily News*. He looked up and took the handkerchief from the breast pocket of his pinstriped jacket. He held it at arm's length as Zee bent to take it from his fingers.

"Ella-Honey, I'm gonna be homeless. Me and Angel out in the street!" Zee sobbed.

This was a spectacle I didn't need. Zee had to go. My loyalty to Dad extended only to moving Cousin Ella—not to Jack, and certainly not to her. I'd never get done with this move if crazy squatters like her from downstairs kept distracting us. But how could I get her out if Cousin Ella continued to coddle her? And still, I couldn't ignore what she said about Dad. What contact did they have when Dad brought Cousin Ella groceries every week? Maybe that's when Zee saw him.

"Ella-Honey, remember when you had those salons? With Langston in town. And Kate Dunham came once. Great dancer, that one! You hid out in the kitchen, like you were fixing drinks. But I knew you really weren't because I didn't hear any glasses tinkling. That's the only time I saw you acting shy. Maybe you didn't think you were good enough to be in her company. I thought you didn't want to see her—or her to see you."

Cousin Ella tightened her jaw and stood over Zee. "Zee, enough . . ."

"Ella-Honey, you were crying up a storm a few weeks ago when you heard Doyle was gone. You said you had to tell Miss Carrie something. I know you didn't do it because she's standing there looking stone dumb. So, let me tell her about her daddy."

This nutty woman was calling me dumb? I couldn't get angry at her. She was too foolish and down-and-out. Cousin Ella just stood silently with her hands in the pockets of her housedress, trying to stare Zee down.

"Yeah, Ella-Honey, that's right. You know when you had those salons, I used to come up and sit here."

She pointed to the chair arm.

"Doyle stood over there where that Miss Carrie is. He always had a Scotch on the rocks in his hand.

Hah! Miss Carrie looks like a prim teetotaler to me. Langston and his, uh, man-friend would sit where Jack is. I used to wear that slit skirt—you know, that black one—so I could hike it up over my knees. I sure had some good legs then. I thought Langston might like them. He was cute. But he didn't even look at me. Didn't say anything, not even hello. His friend gave me the evil eye, though. That was funny."

A disarming cackle came out of her face.

I willed my composure back. "I thought Dad just came here with groceries on his way from work . . ."

They ignored me.

"Yeah, those were some good times," Zee said.

A deep laugh came up from Jack's chest and filled the room. He shook his head at Zee.

Zee's eyes got wide. She toyed with the doilies covering the arms on the chair.

"Jack, are you laughing at me? Langston didn't like me. I don't know why. I didn't do anything to him."

"Zee, you were a young something back then. You didn't know your head from your butt."

"Jack, stop it. You know what sets her off." Cousin Ella moved behind Zee's chair.

Jack persisted. "Ella, you know she'd come up from downstairs every time we had folks here. She must've had nothing to do but have her ear to the door all the time. All she could talk about was how she was channeling Zora Neale. Isn't that right, Zee?"

"Zora Neale Hurston's spirit came to me in a dream. She told me herself that I'm her reincarnate. She gave me a number—152. I played that number—first time

I ever did that—and I won! You remember that don't you, Ella-Honey? I bought that couch with it."

That must have been the raggedy sofa that I saw her on when I came up those stairs.

Jack got a little boy's devilish look on his wrinkled face. "Zee, I bet you never even read her books."

"You think I don't read, huh? I'll bet you that Tiffany lamp! You know, I could sell it and then I could pay some rent somewhere. I wouldn't have to go to the shelter."

He raised his glass toward the bookshelf behind me.

"Carrie, turn around. See that Hurston book behind you?"

I pulled out *Their Eyes Were Watching God*.

"Langston got that first edition signed for Zee. She never bothered to take it downstairs. I don't know how he got that from Zora or even if they were friends then. But I do know, Zee, that you never even looked at it. That's why I kept it." Jack smirked. "He did that for you and you didn't even thank him. And you wonder why he didn't talk to you?"

Cousin Ella, behind Zee, did an emphatic "zip your lip" with her fingers across her mouth toward Jack. Jack didn't respond.

I realized that I'd have to look through every single book before I packed or threw them away to look for valuable first editions and authors' signatures. Everywhere amid the trash there must have been small items of high value. These rooms were filled with trash. I felt overwhelmed.

Jack chuckled to himself. His drink hadn't affected him as much as I thought it would. "Ella, Zee is right. Every month whoever was in town knew they could come here for drinks and Doyle's good cooking. Then we'd talk, maybe even dance to new albums. Sometimes they'd sleep on the couch. I'll never forget when Cab dropped by—just for a hot second—but long enough to do a coupla steps of 'Hi-De-Ho'! He was still wearing zoot suits. Yeah, that was something! Word got out about that, so more guests came to the next month's salon, but Cab never came back."

"Yes, those were good times, yes." Cousin Ella softened her voice when she spoke to Jack. Zee was still sitting, and appeared to be daydreaming.

OK. I'd had enough of this. Yes, I wanted to know more about my dad, but it was 10:45 now. "Listen, we have to deal with getting you ready to move."

I looked directly at Cousin Ella. No one budged. For a moment, the three of them appeared to be in reverie, staring into space.

I scanned the living room for larger items that should be kept. Besides the clock and the lamp, there were a few old African masks and stone statuettes on shelves, small artworks by Romare Bearden on the walls, and the books by Jean Toomer, Claude McKay, Dorothy West, and so many more. Lots of them looked like first editions. That early Jacob Lawrence painting might be museum worthy. And a collector might pay well for the framed letter that Langston signed in green ink. Where to start? I had to focus on my promise to get Cousin Ella out of here, and not on Zee's craziness or Jack's melancholy drinking.

"Hey, Miss Carrie!" Zee suddenly sat bolt upright in her chair.

Now what? What did this woman want from me? By then, Zee was clear-eyed and well over her crying spell.

Cousin Ella stomped toward the door. "Zee, don't you have to see how Angel is doing?"

"Yeah, my baby's baby is coming in three months. We gotta get someplace to live. No little infant baby can live in the street. Not my grandbaby!"

I thought Zee would start crying again, but as Cousin Ella went to open the door, Zee lunged toward me. Jack caught her sweater by the arm as I jumped out of her way. She pulled away from Jack, tripped on the carpet, and yelled at me across the room.

"You think you're something, don't you, Miss Carrie! You don't believe that your daddy used to come here when Ella-Honey had her salons, do you?"

"Cousin Ella, what is she talking about?"

Cousin Ella didn't answer me. She looked calm, as if she had seen this behavior many times.

"Zee, that's enough!"

Zee stood her ground. She looked into the bedroom and saw the suitcase I'd packed.

"So, Ella-Honey, you found a place to go? You didn't even tell me you had plans," Zee said.

Cousin Ella looked at me. "I don't have plans. Carrie does."

I hardly heard any of this because I was too anxious that Zee might come after me again. When her body relaxed, I began to think of my father coming here to Cousin Ella's salons. I'd thought that he was working all those nights. That's what he'd told me. But now I remembered those times when he complained that his paycheck was short. So he was taking time off to come here.

Zee continued to look around. "Well, whatever you're doing they'll take down your door tomorrow, latest the next morning."

She seemed more lucid, momentarily normal.

Cousin Ella looked straight at me. She needed me, that much was becoming clearer. I thought I heard her whisper, "Are you going to come through . . . ?" but I wasn't sure what followed.

Bill flashed in my mind. I had to come through for him, too.

"Listen," Zee said, "Angel and Two-Cent packed up my stuff for me to take to the shelter. They can help you pack, too. And you can help them with a little cash, you know, for their baby."

"Don't ask me. Carrie's the one with the plans."

"You really mean Miss Carrie's the one with the cash. No problem for her to pay them. Right, Miss Carrie?" She was sneering at me.

The longer I saw Zee, the more I believed Cousin Ella that there was no way Dad would be interested in this foolish woman. I knew he wouldn't have tolerated the way she smelled. But, who knows, maybe she didn't have water in what was left of her apartment.

Zee didn't wait for me to answer if I could pay Angel and Two-Cent, whoever they were. She sauntered into the kitchen and came back with a glass. She held it out to Jack, who poured her a drink and topped off his own. She sat next to him on the sofa. Now all three of them seemed to be staring at their shoes, waiting for what I might decide.

Their eyes were following my hands as I folded them in front of me. I took a deep breath. I was sure they knew that there was no way I could do all this work in an hour. It would take a few days, at least, to move them. I did need help. I had to get to the lawyer's office by two o'clock to sign away my condo. Bill would be waiting for me there. Maybe these young people could help get this done.

"Who are Angel and, who's the other one, Two-Cent?" I asked Zee, but she was too busy sipping her drink to answer me.

Finally, Cousin Ella sat up. "Angel is eighteen and pregnant. Two-Cent is the twenty-year-old who got her that way."

Zee perked up. "Don't talk about my Angel like that!"

"I'm just stating facts."

Cousin Ella said, "Carrie, they're good kids. Hire them."

With that, Zee stood up and gulped her drink. I was ready to defend myself with the heavy metal statuette on the floor if she lunged at me again—but she didn't. Instead she walked toward the front door and said, "I'll get them."

Cousin Ella said, "Go on ahead, Zee."

Jack glanced at Zee with his drink half raised.

Zee was agitated again. Her body was shaking as she tipped her head toward me. Then she ran out into the noisy hallway. Cousin Ella slowly got up and locked the door.

I was used to working with a staff of competent people who scheduled their days in planner diaries. We organized our projects with logical outlines. We met our goals. My secretary clearly pronounced consonants when she answered the phone. I wore business suits and tailored dresses. My desk was neat. I was cordial and very good at getting donors to give up funds. But here? How could I make sense out of this clutter with the help of a hapless crew—Zee, Angel, and Two-Cent?

Chapter 6

I saw then that Dad couldn't have been just in the guise of daddy do-good dutifully bringing groceries to poor relations. And from what I'd just heard from Cousin Ella, I knew he came here more often after I told him that I was going out again with Bill. That was after the dance audition fiasco.

I had more questions, but I had to immediately assess if Angel and Two-Cent could finish the mounds of trash and wearable clothes that I had sorted and piled up in the bedroom. Inside, yes, it was still chaotic, but except for horns in the street, at least there was no construction noise.

I realized it was lunchtime when I looked out the living room window facing the street. Four workers were sitting on the stoop eating sandwiches and drinking coffee. A pretty young woman with perfectly done long braids and a yoga mat rolled in her backpack walked by quickly. One of the men said something, no doubt crude, that was drowned out by traffic sounds.

I suddenly had a flash of my younger self. I, too, had rushed here and there, and where had it led? Here?

Through the dirty window, I could see that the Harlem skyline had changed since I was a girl. I saw a few new high-rise buildings against the hazy sky. I could see construction crews on adjacent blocks. Just as Cousin Ella and Jack, those old residents had to move. As they left, many had neither family nor living friends to help them. I saw the rooftops where I had so much fun when my mother and her friend Deloris would make a swing from a clothesline on the pipes on the roof. I loved the rhythm of the swing. I pumped so hard that Mom was afraid I'd fly off the building. Now those rooftops were lifeless. Many of the residents who stayed were losing their lifeline, their sense of community.

I felt someone behind me. I turned from the window to find Cousin Ella standing with her hands on her hips.

"Why haven't you called him yet? Carrie? Don't you have to tell him you might be late for your appointment?"

"Who? Bill? No, not yet."

"Why not?"

I felt like she was looking through me.

"You'll sort it out with him."

Sort Bill out? I didn't know why I had no answer for her. Usually I was in constant contact with Bill. We shared everything, almost everything—shopping lists, meeting schedules, sometimes current events. But now I didn't know how to explain to him why I'd spent time listening to Zee. Or why I was beginning to care about Cousin Ella, or even Jack. Or why I felt ambivalent about tossing out Cousin Ella's dancing shoes. No, I wasn't ready to talk to him.

And Cousin Ella would not allow me a moment's peace. She kept buzzing around me everywhere I went in the apartment. She motioned me toward the bedroom and closed the door.

"Carrie, where are you moving us?" Her voice was soft with a touch of sadness.

Finally, I could discuss business with her about the reality of her situation.

"Well, first, Dad told me to make arrangements for you only."

"Only me? But Doyle knew Jack. He saw him all the time."

"He didn't leave any instructions about Jack."

She paused a long minute before she said, "OK. Then I know for sure I'm not going. They'll have to drag us out of here."

"You can't mean that . . ."

"I'm ninety-five years old. I'm not going to be hanging around much longer, anyway. So, I mean that. They'll just have to carry us out."

Carry them out? "What are you saying?"

"Who's to say that I wouldn't be in a safe place, no matter how I leave here?"

"Cousin Ella, you know that I made a promise to Dad to get you to a safe place."

"Yeah, I know. I made a promise to Doyle, too, for you." She picked up a cross pendant from the bed that

I hadn't seen before and put it in her pocket. I must have been sitting on it after the ceiling flooded. "This was my mother's. I took it off her neck when she died. I always carry it with me, just in case."

With what she said about being "carried out," I began to be supersensitive to what I was seeing and hearing. Why was Jack grinning on the sofa with a drink in his hand? Why didn't Cousin Ella help me with the sorting and packing? Yes, she was a little slow, but she didn't seem to have any major infirmities. Actually, for her age, she seemed to be quite strong. Strong enough to hurt herself—or Jack—I didn't know. I'd have to watch her as closely as she was watching me.

Cousin Ella went over to the dusty blue dresser, pulled the ornate brass handle on the curvy top drawer. One side of the handle snapped off, but she managed to get out an old photo album with a quilted brown cover that was stuffed amid perfume bottles and talcum powder.

"I want to show you this. Let's go sit with Jack."

"Won't Angel and Two-Cent be coming up soon to help?"

She laughed. "Zee doesn't remember anything one minute to the next. Maybe they'll show up, maybe not."

"I do need to call Bill."

I thought of Bill pacing the condo's three rooms, sitting on boxes that we'd neatly stacked around the walls. I'd wanted him to help me. When I asked him, he told me that Cousin Ella was my problem, not his. He said he had business to take care of. I figured the "business" was saying goodbye to the young redhead who owned a larger condo upstairs from mine. I saw how she would always smile at him in the building's lobby. I never cared about that. I ignored it. That was his business. I wondered if he would find more "business" to take care of in Seattle. Would I care about it there? I knew I would be isolated until I could find my own friends.

"Carrie?"

How long had I been drifting from the work at hand?

"You will call him. There's time."

"OK. I'll take a look—but only five minutes."

She pushed me out of the bedroom, then toward the end seat on the sofa. She sat between me and Jack. That made me feel anxious, trapped. I wanted Zee's two young people to help me. Otherwise it would take me a week to finish with Cousin Ella. A week! I had to leave for Seattle the next night. No, I couldn't sit around with these old people. I had to call Bill.

When I started to get up, Cousin Ella touched my thigh and motioned for me to sit down. She smiled. "You still got a dancer's legs, you know."

Until a few years ago, I did feel good working out to music, jazz especially, a few days a week. Though I knew it was too late for me to even think about dancing professionally—I'd certainly felt my age when I lugged those suitcases upstairs—even now I really enjoyed doing a fifteen-minute dance routine once in a while. And there was Bill. He had liked the way I kept myself fit, and I liked making him happy with my body. But when Dad got sick and Bill started talking about looking for a job away from New York, I started stress snacking and skipping workouts. I was still living with the weight that resulted.

Cousin Ella got her busy fingers piecing together the torn pages in the album. Jack put down his drink, squeezed his arm around me to touch her shoulder, and mumbled "Hmm, hmm, hmm" when he saw the photos.

"OK, Carrie. I want you to see this." She plopped down in her lap the album she had just organized.

I glanced over at the many small black-and-white photos with brown edges that were pasted on faded black sheets of construction paper. I was curious. OK, sure, I could take a few minutes to indulge her.

She covered some photos on the page with her hand and pointed to the one of my father as a round-faced, curly-haired little boy in stylishly tapered short pants. Next to him was a young woman in a white sundress with Marcelled curls. Cousin Ella held the photo up to her face, covering the scarred side.

"Yeah, that's me and Doyle. Hard to believe? That was way back in the twenties right after I came back from Paris the first time. I was hardly grown. Had to take care of Mama's business after she passed. She left me enough to go back to France. With her gone, there was nothing to keep me here."

"You both looked so innocent . . ."

"Are you talking about Ella?" Jack had a sly smile.

Cousin Ella continued, "Around then your

grandmama told me that they named him Doyle because your granddaddy, who was a Pullman porter, met Arthur Conan Doyle—you know, Sherlock Holmes—on a train."

That was amusing to me. "So Dad was born a mystery?"

Jack laughed. "Who isn't?"

Cousin Ella was serious.

"Those were hard times, Carrie. Yeah, those years between the wars had hard times like I hope you never know. But Doyle was just a boy. He would take his shoeshine box over to the park to try to make some money for his parents. Y'know, he made that shoebox himself."

"Carrie wouldn't know about hard times. Looks like she's doing all right for herself, looks like she's well-off to me." Jack's speech was a bit slurred, but coherent.

Was he trying to make me feel guilty for doing well? If he was—and Zee, too—it wouldn't work. How did I get what I have? By trading dancing for an office job.

Cousin Ella turned the page.

"Well, look at this! Here I was the next year."

"The lovely stellar Miss Ella!" Jack had perked up.

This photo was on a page by itself. Cousin Ella, when her face was clear and beautiful, was sitting at a restaurant table with her legs crossed high on her hip, surrounded by two men in wide-lapel suits. One of them was a younger Jack. The waiter, holding a napkin, looked familiar.

"Who . . . ?"

"Don't you know that's Langston? That was him working—waiting tables, cooking, doing whatever he could do to be in Paris. But I told you he was smart. He knew he was a writer. He already knew Spanish from when he was in Mexico, living with his father. With the French he learned there, he could translate Jacques Roumain's poetry."

"Dad knew French, too."

"Yeah, OK. He learned some when his ship went into Marseilles. You know those Army men. They'd learn enough to say some sweet nothings to all those French women who were flinging their panties around. At least to those women who talked to the men, the ones who didn't think black men were animals with tails like they had been warned. Who knows? Maybe some of those women wanted a look-see to find out for themselves." She giggled to herself.

Jack said, "Ella, you know they got more than a look-see. Maybe even a few dollars for their, um, curiosity."

I was getting the impression that Jack and Cousin Ella were more than suited for each other. But the grief for Dad that I had been holding back was beginning to well up again.

"Not my dad. He didn't do that."

She looked at me out of the corner of her eye.

"No, not Doyle. He was always faithful to Janie. I know it. Zee sure tried. But then, after he did those portraits she asked for, Doyle wouldn't give her the time of day."

"You know your dad didn't like that Langston was hanging out with those Lefty writers. You know, like Guillen, Roumain, McKay—lots of others. And Doyle really didn't like that Langston went to the Soviet Union. Doyle looked all that up and it made him very leery of Langston."

"Maybe he thought Langston had gone too far, or maybe he envied his courage. You know that last week I got Dad's folded flag for his service as a vet. He might have had lots of complaints about this country, but he fought for it."

"Yeah. Doyle had courage himself. When he got home he carried that gun he got in the war. When he and your granddaddy were on a train to Virginia and were told they had to ride in a segregated car, your dad wanted to shoot somebody. To him, he hadn't fought and risked his life for this country to ride in a second-class train car. He almost created a ruckus. Good thing your granddaddy was still strong enough to quiet him."

"I never saw him do anything like that."

"He never did that again. He knew he'd never be a good family man unless he calmed down, and he really wanted to marry Janie. But I knew that war had changed him."

"I only knew him as he was . . . my dad."

"I know. But whenever he could, Doyle talked about being overseas. Sometimes I think he thought he was better than Langston because he had been an Army sergeant. But Langston got fed up with it and blurted out that I'd told him about Doyle working to organize a labor union when he was a young man. Some people saw that organizing as subversive, too."

Cousin Ella sat up straight to tell me, "One night Doyle got fed up with that and said, 'Langston, you are nothing but a fat-ass pencil pusher.'"

Jack chimed in. "Yeah, I remember that. Langston shot back, 'And you were just big-butt cannon fodder.'"

"Doyle thought he'd really get him with 'And you can't make a commitment in a relationship!'"

Jack added, "Langston's man-friend cringed with that. Langston didn't want Doyle to get away with that so he pushed. 'You couldn't even commit to do more of those little drawings—even when Romare said he'd help you.'"

"Doyle was sensitive about that artwork and Langston saw he was getting to him, so he wouldn't let Doyle be. He dug in. 'And you say you know French?'" Cousin Ella was enjoying this. She looked like a naughty schoolgirl.

Jack said, "Doyle came back, 'I do.'"

"Langston kept at it. 'Then let me hear you say something.'"

"Well, Carrie, your dad got this mischievous smile on his face and narrowed his eyes at Langston. He came out with 'Voulez-vous coucher avec moi, ce soir?'"

Cousin Ella said that with a good French accent, as if she herself had said it many times before.

"We all gasped. Then Langston started laughing, very heartily. Doyle joined in. Before you knew it, we were all holding our bellies from laughing so hard."

Jack put down his glass. "Yeah, then Langston said

to Doyle, 'Cousin, let's dance.' Then I got up and put on one of our old 78s—'Hey-Ba-Ba-Re-Bop.'"

"Next thing we knew, Doyle gulped down half his drink, then he got up and danced the Lindy with Langston! We all clapped to the music and cheered them on. When it was over, they hugged like two long-lost friends."

"Dad used to like dancing with Mom. But with another man? I can't imagine Dad doing that."

Cousin Ella pulled me back to the photo album.

"Why not? They were cousins. You have lots to learn, Carrie. Lots you don't know."

Cousin Ella flipped to the back of the album.

"Look, here's a napkin where Langston wrote some notes. I guess he was starting a poem."

I suddenly got interested in the value of the photos and artifacts in the album.

"Meanwhile, back home . . ."—she had fun with that build-up—"your dad was marrying Janie."

She revealed a photo of my father about fifteen years older than he was in the little-boy photo. He was in an Army sergeant uniform with a big grin, hugging his young, beautiful wife: my mother in a short, front-buttoned wedding dress and small flowered hat.

"That dress was nothing special. Just plain blue. I guess it was the best she could do during the war."

After all these years, Cousin Ella was still getting digs into my mother. I didn't think she knew how hurtful that was to me.

I didn't know why I'd never seen that photo, or any image of their wedding. I couldn't contain myself. Tears started flowing. My parents were so happy then. I thought of what the years had done to them. Mother's beautiful body crushed in the car crash to a bloody pulp! Her spirit was strong, though. She held on for a week in the ICU. We thought and prayed that she would overcome her injuries and get better. Dad told them it was OK to move her to that nursing home. It was the place attached to the assisted living building where I had to take Cousin Ella. How could I bear to see that place again? But Mom, she was with us a while longer, until she started going down. They asked Dad if she should go back to the hospital. It was the first and only time I saw him cry. Then he said, "No, she's suffered enough." I was just fourteen. I needed my mother, but we stayed with her and watched her die in that nursing home. I had that recurrent nightmare.

"Yeah, baby, I know how you feel." Cousin Ella held my hands. "They're both gone. It's just us chickens now."

She was cheerful and I began to calm down. Jack was back to sipping his drink. Cousin Ella skipped a few more pages, then nudged me with her elbow to look at more.

Out of the corner of my eye, I saw that it was 11:30. My stomach tensed. I had to leave in two hours at the latest, but I didn't get up to pack. I wanted to see more.

The next photo was a group shot on the very sofa where I was sitting. There were a few drinks on the side tables. I recognized Cab Calloway sitting in the middle seat. He didn't have the big smile he was known for in his acts. He had a polite, let's-get-this-over-with smile. Langston was sitting to his right. The curtains were open and light was streaming in, making his eyes sparkle. A man I didn't know was standing behind him with his hand on Langston's shoulder. Two women were seated on Cab's other side—one in the seat, the other next to her seated on the sofa's arm.

"Who are they?"

Jack was quick to respond. "Them? They were the Martha's Vineyard ladies."

"Yeah. Dorothy West and Lois Jones. They met here for a few days when Lois got back from France. Hmmm. Or was she going there? She was always going somewhere to present her art."

Then I noticed a man's shadow in the corner of the photo. I looked more closely and saw that it was Dad standing there looking on. I recognized his tweed sports jacket, the one he wore to work.

Cousin Ella let me linger on that page. "I think Doyle had just brought us a box of groceries. He had to rush out because he said he was late for his shift. You know, Carrie, he was working nights to make more money to pay for you to stay in college."

"That's what he told me."

After Mom died, he'd made a point of reminding me constantly that he was sacrificing for me. But he was supporting Cousin Ella and Jack, too, by bringing them food. He told me this should be what relatives do for each other. Judging from this photo, though, maybe if they'd spent less on booze, they would have had more for food. Were they taking advantage of his good will?

"Doyle would run in with our groceries, put them in the fridge. Sometimes he'd watch us. I think that's what he was doing over there in the corner where you were Carrie. He'd just stand there ogling us—didn't say much. Then, next thing I'd know, he'd be gone. I guess he had to get the subway to work down at the post office on 33rd. At least that's how he was for a while."

Jack put his drink on the table. "Maybe he just thought we were too crazy. You remember, all those show folks we used to have here . . . "

"Yeah, but you know he didn't act that way for too long. He could've just been shy at first, especially around Langston—maybe, too, around any of us who'd been to Paris."

"What do you mean, 'at first'?"

I knew that my father would sometimes let off steam by hanging out with some coworkers at a local bar after the night shift. But I was trying to imagine my father—with his shined shoes, white shirts, single-breasted sports coats, and a government paycheck—encountering Cousin Ella's artsy friends. After all, he was the man who didn't want me to be a dancer.

As soon as she started to turn the page, Cousin Ella abruptly slammed the album shut. She must have heard the footsteps in the hall before I did. Then there was a light knocking on the door accompanied by a man's soft voice.

"*Abuelita, abuelita!*"

Cousin Ella went to the door. This time she didn't bother to put the chain on before she fully opened it. A tan-faced construction worker stood there, almost as tall as the doorframe. She motioned him in. From across the room, I could smell his day-old sweat rising above the hallway stench that I had gotten used to.

"*Abuelita*, tomorrow we'll be on this floor. You're next. *Entiendes?*"

"Felix, would you like some coffee?" Cousin Ella walked toward the kitchen.

I must have looked puzzled, because Jack said to me, "Ella just likes that young man's attention."

"No, not now, *gracias*. I have to get back to work." He gently bowed his head.

"Just a minute. I have something for you."

He stood waiting in the doorway.

Cousin Ella went into the kitchen. I saw her searching through a drawer. She brought out a wrinkled folder and gave it to Felix.

Jack's face hardened. Felix smudged a dark fingerprint on the stiff manila folder.

Felix read slowly. "'*Un sueño diferido*' and '*Yo también, canto a América.*'" For a moment, he was speechless. Then he said, "*Abuelita*, you're giving me these?"

Jack said, "Yeah, Ella. What are you doing? Those are signed translations of Langston's poems."

By reflex, I moved to grab them back from Felix, but stopped short of Cousin Ella's hand. She was matter-of-fact about the papers.

"What good are they doing for us?" she asked Jack.

"OK, sure. They're yours to do with what you want." Jack had lost his cordial demeanor.

Felix took a little notepad and short pencil out of his shirt pocket. As he was writing, he told Cousin Ella, "This number is Hector's, *mi hermano*. Tomorrow he can help you move. But you've got to get your stuff ready."

Cousin Ella smiled toward Jack, folded the paper, and put it in her pocket.

Felix was jumpy. "I have to get back to work. I'm not supposed to be here. *Muchas gracias!*" He rushed into the hall with the folder in his fist. With the filth in the hallways, I hated to think of where he would put it while he worked.

Cousin Ella tilted her head toward me. "So, Carrie, don't you think you'd better make that call to Bill?"

"Yes."

She nodded. I went into the bedroom for privacy and shut the door.

I had to let Bill know what I was dealing with. He'd be leaving my condo for the lawyer's appointment in about an hour. It had been my place for over a decade. I was the one who had to sign the documents to sell it. I needed to be alone to gather my thoughts away from Cousin Ella's chaos. I knew the truth was that I'd miss the appointment with the lawyer.

CHAPTER 7

✦

I WAS DREADING MAKING THE CALL. Bill was impossible when anyone didn't follow his plan, and at this point, I had no counterplan of my own to offer him. Usually I could come up with some contingency before his predictable outbursts, so I had to get settled by taking a few minutes to mindfully search the sopping bed, the moth-eaten clothes, hoping to discover anything that I could of Cousin Ella's and Jack's lives that would give me any tangible clues that could seed a plan.

I thought of how Dad didn't teach me how to change, though change does happen no matter how we try to stop it. I married and moved, but he never left the apartment he raised me in. To him, it was a shrine to Mom. He kept all her furnishings just as she had left them. Nothing could be out of place. I had taken for granted that every day of Dad's life had been predictable—a life based on the schedule of his workweek. But after meeting Zee, I wasn't sure. I was sure that Dad cared about me and Cousin Ella—who knows, and maybe Jack, too. But standing in the clutter of the bedroom, I knew that I was mired in dead history. I had to find a way forward. They and I had to move. We had no choice.

From the far corner in the bedroom, I could look into the living room and see them. Jack's hands shook as he fingered through LP music albums and a few ancient 78s. His eyes had been flashing alert when Zee was here. Now, as Cousin Ella went to him to help choose an album, his eyes lingered on her face and the movement of her hands.

Suddenly, there was a loud bang from the demolition work downstairs. I nearly jumped out of my skin. Cousin Ella and Jack didn't respond to it, though the sound muffled whatever music they were playing. I guessed they, in their nineties, had weathered so much suffering that a mere loud sound was of no consequence to them. They chose to play "Do Nothin' Till You Hear from Me" and went back to the sofa holding hands.

With so much work to do in their apartment, I didn't understand their denial of the situation. Yes, they were frail, but they really could do something to help themselves, like take the small paintings and drawings from the wall right next to them.

It was almost noon. I had to stop procrastinating. I had to talk to Bill. He deserved an update. I wasn't behaving like the executive wife that he was used to. That take-charge Carrie would've come in here, packed a few nightgowns and housedresses, then pulled Cousin Ella onto the street into a taxi. I'd have demanded my gift. I'd have been done with this within an hour. She'd already be in her new assisted-living studio. That's what Bill expected of me.

As for Jack, well, he wasn't part of my posthumous promise to Dad. Since Dad didn't mention Jack, Jack would've just been on his own. Sure, Cousin Ella might have kicked and screamed, but she was a helpless old lady. She'd have to deal with the reality of her plight. After all, I was doing a favor for her. That would have been the way businesslike Carrie would have done this, but for some reason I didn't feel like my usual self. As of yesterday, when I'd quit my job, I'd felt unmoored without a title, fending for myself.

I went to the window and I watched people on the street walk around the dumpster in front of the building. I took a breath and called Bill.

"Hel—No, I'm not done yet . . . I know I should be there already . . . if you'll be quiet for a minute, I'll explain . . . The buyers said what? . . . No, I don't want to lose the sale . . . Of course I know my priorities. One of them is what I'm doing here."

My business degree was kicking in. I was the executive. He was the engineer. This was a staff meeting.

"They want to do this by four? . . . Listen, I might be able to get there by then . . . Well, I'm sorry that 'might' isn't good enough! . . . No, I'm not letting you down . . . How many times do you have to remind me? Yes! You did the down payment on the new house. Yes! You expect me to pay my part—and, yes, I have to sell my condo."

Blah, blah, blah.

"OK. Call the lawyer. Tell them to wait. I'll be there
. . . Yes, I will!"

I paused. He didn't respond to me. Finally, he
slammed down the phone. I had no time to say "love
you," and right then, I thought it was just as well that
I didn't.

I loved the condo that I'd owned for twelve years.
Dad was right that my business degree would open
doors. It opened my condo door every day. I loved
decorating it with art I got from small galleries all over
Manhattan, from Greenwich Village to Harlem. Those
pieces were crated up and waiting to be loaded on the
long-haul moving truck the next morning.

I thought about twenty years ago, when Dad invited
Bill to our apartment, Bill brought some Chinese take-
out. I remembered that it was bland noodles Dad tried
to spice up with lots of soy sauce. When Dad went
for the chopsticks and Bill for a fork, Dad used a fork.
Dad stifled a yawn when Bill described his five-year
plan, starting with a degree in engineering, a double
masters in business and engineering, and a managerial
job, which would lead to future advancement. When
Bill left, Dad said, "I hope he asks to marry you." I was
a college student who loved dancing. I wasn't thinking
of marriage. I was concerned that Bill would be the
type of guy who would want a family—according to
his five-year plan. I didn't know what would happen to
my body if I became pregnant.

I looked out at Cousin Ella and Jack. They were finishing a slow dance to an impossibly scratchy 78-rpm

version of Duke Ellington's "Do Nothin' Till You Hear From Me." They both had big smiles as they moved in a tiny space in the living room. I remembered that Duke was one of my dad's favorites. Dad prided himself on having every album Ellington ever made. Sometimes at night, when he was at work, I'd put on those albums and make up dance routines. That's when I fantasized about being a choreographer. In the bedroom corner, hidden from their view, I danced a few of the steps I remembered from those routines. The movement was soothing after talking with Bill.

The next record dropped and I heard Sidney Bechet's "Blues My Naughty Sweetie Gives to Me." It was faster than the Ellington piece. When I went into the living room, I saw that Jack's cane was on the sofa and he was leaning on Ella. They were dancing jerkily, as fast as their old legs would let them. Actually, they kept up with the beat very well. In that living room with its many decades-old artifacts, they could have been dancing in Paris or Harlem in their heyday.

I couldn't resist. When I started moving my body to the music, Cousin Ella grinned and motioned to me to join them. She took my hand and Jack leaned on my shoulder and hers. He smelled of the whiskey he'd been sipping all day. I stepped slightly faster than they did, which disrupted their rhythms. I slowed down. When I looked up, the framed photo of Langston was smiling at us.

At the end of the song, Jack was panting. He held on to Cousin Ella's hand as he sat back down in the armchair. She smiled at me.

"You're earning it."

"What?"

"Your gift, Carrie. Did you forget?"

Though I answered her, "No, of course, not," it occurred to me that, with so much going on during the morning, I *had* forgotten what I wanted for myself. Curiosity about that promised gift, after all, was part of my motivation for getting into the taxi this morning.

Cousin Ella sat at the end of the sofa and patted the seat next to her for me to sit. She had the photo album on her lap again. Since I had no doubt that I was already too late to get to the lawyer, I didn't really care. I thought it was OK to take a few more minutes to relax. Jack leaned forward in his chair so he, too, could see the photos as she flipped pages I'd already seen. Cousin Ella wasn't in any of the photos. I had the impression that she was always the photographer. That was probably her strategy to avoid showing her scar in the photos. The only photos I ever saw of her were taken when she was young and beautiful.

She turned the next page while she looked directly at me. So did Jack. I saw a full-page photo. There, in crisp black-and-white, Dad was sitting in the middle of the sofa—where I was—with a big drink in his hand. To his left was Langston, and to his right was a man with a round face who I didn't know. They were all grinning. A much younger and prettier Zee, in a dark dress, was standing behind Dad, looking down on the men with her face tightly pursed. The nice-looking man in a light shirt next to her, who had his hand on

Langston's shoulder, was the same man in the other photo. Jack was at the far end, raising a drink.

"Who's this?" I pointed to the round face.

Cousin Ella said, "Romare, Romare Bearden. He and your dad got along fine. Romare had gone to France during the war like your dad. They knew no one else wanted to hear about it, so they would sometimes go off in a corner and talk about those Army experiences."

"Really? I thought Dad only did that with Mr. Jackson."

"Romare liked to hear your dad tell him about when he was ordered to raise the flag. He was overseas in some camp during the war. Your dad told his superior there was no rope and nothing else to raise that flag. Again, he ordered Doyle to raise it. So Doyle found some detonator wire to put up that flag. Now you know that didn't go over well. But what could a young officer do? Doyle had followed orders."

Jack laughed until tears were in his eyes. But that story wasn't amusing to me. I couldn't imagine Dad doing anything even mildly rebellious. He was the dad who was so precise that he forced me to make square corners with the sheets when I made up my bed.

Jack added, "Your dad loved talking to him about art, too. Romare was doing those collages—those scenes with black folks, you know like that little one over there. Some of them were even in museums. Doyle told Romare he'd taken a drawing class and Romare looked at some of his drawings. He encouraged Doyle even though I knew—we all knew—they

91

really weren't that good. They were OK, but not nearly as good as Romare's."

Cousin Ella was still inspecting my face.

"If your dad'd had more practice or had gone to a few classes, he could have been just as good—and he knew it."

I'm not sure I believed that. Was she just trying to be nice?

Jack said, "But Doyle was shy around most of us."

"Yeah. At first he would stand back and watch us—like we were some zoo specimens living in a world he didn't understand. But I grew up with him. I knew he was like us at heart. You know, he used to carve sailboats when he was a boy. They were good enough to sell. But instead he'd sneak over to Harlem Meer in Central Park and set them sailing to enjoy himself. That was the most fun he had when he was a boy."

"He did a lot of that woodwork, fixed our kitchen cabinets when the super wouldn't. Yeah, Doyle was industrious."

"Jack liked that so he wouldn't have to fix it himself. But the only time Doyle got on a real ship was when the Army sent him over to Marseilles. He told me once about coming into that port with the sun shining bright on the water. He looked at that really good. With the war, he thought it might be the last time he'd see the sun."

"I've always wanted to go to the Riviera, to see what Dad saw . . ."

Cousin Ella burst out laughing.

"Carrie, Carrie! The Riviera? You don't know

how easy things have been for you! You want to go to a French beach? Buy a plane ticket and a bikini." She looked at me and shook her head. I couldn't see myself in something that skimpy. I didn't think she could either.

"Naw, he sure couldn't talk to you, or for that matter, any of us, about the war. That's why he and Romare got along so well. They were both relieved to get those horrors they'd seen out of their systems. Yeah, your dad had his friend Mr. Jackson across the street, did talk about the war, but mainly they just drank and felt sorry for themselves because they were widowers. Jackson didn't know anything about art."

"But Langston was in that photo, too. What did he have to say about all this?"

Cousin Ella glanced at Langston's face in the photo.

"Langston didn't say that much to Doyle about wartime, because he didn't want to talk about when he was reporting on the Spanish Civil War. Doyle thought that just meant Langston wrote stories. But it was dangerous covering a war. Maybe it was around then that he translated García Lorca—that poor young poet who was finished off with a firing squad. Anyway, your dad wouldn't have been much interested in Langston's war reports. To him, writing about it wasn't the same as ducking bullets. Besides, to Doyle it was the Spaniards' problem, not America's."

"Why not?"

"You don't get it, do you, Carrie? Langston didn't have to fight to the death like Doyle did in the Black Forest. You remember that your dad had a scar on his lip from that German's bayonet. He killed that man. I'd hear him rant, sometimes cry, to Romare about what it meant to kill a man you don't even know, because of some orders you don't understand, for a country that tells you to get in the back of the bus. He wondered if that man had a wife and daughter to go home to like he did. He'd reminisce about being in that famous 369th Infantry. You know the one from that armory a few blocks up the street? Romare had been in the 372nd. Both of them knew what it was like to be in all-black regiments. So Doyle and Romare listened to each other. I think Romare wanted to talk about the war as much as your dad wanted to talk about art some days."

I thought of the photo of Dad's unit. The long sheet of the faded sepia images of black soldiers standing behind white officers. I wondered how he felt watching black American soldiers die in that indignity of a segregated unit in a war to free Europeans.

Jack perked up, leaned toward me. "He told all of us about how he and his men had to help clean up one of those concentration camps. Dachau, I think."

Cousin Ella added, "When he told us that, he looked like his heart was wrenched from his body."

"Yeah. He'd drink more, too, when he talked about it. A coupla times he had to sleep all night right here on this sofa."

"Dad was here? Not at work?"

Jack leaned back. He sunk into the worn-out sofa pillows.

"Doyle told us about the stench of it. How, as they got closer to the camp, the smell of burning flesh and filth overwhelmed his men. He knew there was no way that those local German people didn't know what was happening in that awful place. He tried to figure out why they didn't speak up. Were they afraid for themselves? Did they believe what was happening—killing all those people for nothing—was right?"

Cousin Ella was breathing fast.

"Doyle constantly asked how could anyone do that to other humans. He knew that evil wasn't black or white. But he knew it was right to free the people who'd survived in that camp. And then he came home to Janie and you—and news of black veterans being lynched. I could tell he was angry."

"He never talked to me about that."

I imagined those photos of Dad in his Army uniform. He was always smiling. He was supposed to smile to keep peace in Mom's heart and his mother's. How could he show them his suffering? Was it the same with me—that he wanted to keep me safe?

Cousin Ella looked stern.

"Why would he talk to you? He knew that all you wanted to do was dance. You were a kid who only thought about what you wanted to do. You wouldn't have understood. It took all his energy to keep you under control so he could raise you to be self-sufficient. He didn't want you to wind up being a poor old woman like me with nothing but some old clothes and a few paintings. But, y'know, I still have my dignity left."

I couldn't listen to this. "How would he or anyone else know what I could understand? I wasn't, and am not, stupid."

Cousin Ella smirked. "But you weren't wise. I don't know if you are even now."

Before I could respond, Jack added, "Ella, I'm just going to straight-out tell her. Your dad liked coming to our salons."

They gave me a few seconds to be quiet, to try to absorb what they were saying. I was staring at the photo. Dad always told me how hard he worked for me, how he worked nights and had no social life because he wanted to be a good single father. Yet here he was, drinking, smiling, and socializing. Now it made sense to me why some mornings, when I'd be leaving for class, he'd come home looking withdrawn and like he'd slept in his clothes. I didn't know how to process what Cousin Ella and Jack were telling me.

Then we all heard loud women's voices in the hallway and a knock at the door. Cousin Ella got up to answer it. She didn't primp or put the chain lock on this time. I followed her. Jack silently took the album from the sofa and stuck it between the chair arm and seat cushion where he sat. He seemed to be hiding it. I wanted to take another look at those photos, but when Cousin Ella opened the door, two young people were standing there. A pregnant young woman in a tight green T-shirt and jeans and a skinny young man in an extra-large City College logo sweatshirt and short dreadlocks.

Cousin Ella let them in. Zee came rushing in after them.

"Miss Carrie, this is Angel."

The young woman briefly looked at Cousin Ella's scar. She said "Hi," and sized me up and down.

"And Two-Cent."

He ignored Zee and nodded toward me. "I'm Jimmy Green, Miss Carrie. So, what do you want us to do?'

Angel spoke up. "Wait, Two-Cent. She didn't tell us if she's paying us."

I offered them minimum wage for the rest of the day, maybe through the next morning.

Angel shook her head. "That's all you're paying us to clean up this mess?"

I offered a dollar an hour more, and Two-Cent—or Jimmy—shook my hand.

"Deal."

Angel gave him a dirty look. So did Zee. I guessed they still didn't think it was enough. That morning, in my rush, I hadn't had time to get cash at the bank. So they had to accept that this was all I could offer them.

Two-Cent was tall, over six feet. He had a piercing, focused look.

I asked him what he'd like to be called.

"Jimmy." He said this softly and half smiled.

I told Jimmy Two-Cent to go to the liquor store that I'd seen down the street when I got out of the taxi. I wanted him to get as many boxes as he could.

Jack didn't miss a beat. He fished in his pocket for a few bills.

"Well, since you're going that way, bring me back another bottle of this whiskey." Jack pointed to the label. Jimmy Two-Cent took the money on his way out the door, then we heard him running down the staircase.

Zee finally spoke up. "And what can Angel do? Nothing too hard for my baby."

Angel had well-developed arm muscles. Even with her pregnancy, I knew that she could do more than Zee would allow, but I didn't want to set off a crazy woman. Zee followed me when I led Angel into the bedroom. "You can fold these clothes, then pack them when Jimmy, Two-Cent, comes back with the boxes."

Zee's eyes widened. "Look at all that, would'ya? Ella knew I needed some clothes, but she kept all this to herself."

Zee held an iridescent, sequined cocktail dress to her shoulders and wiggled.

"Oh, yuck! Roaches!" She tossed the dress, with its new hatch of baby roaches, across the room.

Angel ducked and cut her eyes at her mother, then looked to me.

"Mama calls him Two-Cent because she says he don't have two cents to rub together to take care of me and this baby."

Zee said, "Yeah, college boyfriend don't have nothing."

The leak had mostly dried, but an ominous damp circle remained. The plaster could fall in at any time. I moved Angel from under it and she started folding the 1940s blouses in the nearest pile. As I walked out of the room, I heard her laughing at the old-fashioned collars and sleeves.

Zee, who continued to lurk in the bedroom, told Angel, "They got bad mojo in here!" then quickly left the room.

"Mom, you don't believe in that old-timey superstition, do you?" Angel giggled.

I didn't care what was in there, juju or whatever. Now that I had workers—who I was paying—I wanted to keep track of their hours. I noted on a paper scrap in my purse that Angel and Jimmy Two-Cent started at noon. I double-checked the cash in my wallet.

"Zee."

She took her sweet time to answer. She had already plopped down on the sofa and was asking Jack for a drink. The bottle was empty. Jack must have finished it. I was surprised that he was able to keep his eyes open wide enough to ogle Zee's legs.

"Yes, Miss Carrie?"

"Would you get us some pizza?" I offered her cash.

She jumped up and was out of the apartment faster than I'd seen her move all morning.

Cousin Ella took Zee's seat. "I hope we see her again. I'm getting hungry."

She turned toward Langston's photo on the wall, then to me.

"You know why he used to come here?"

"Because you were his cousin . . ."

"Well, I guess that was it."

"And you had your salons."

"He had many other friends besides us who he could and did visit for good company. A lot of writers, but regular folk, too."

She motioned to Jack to take the photo album out from the side of the seat. She flipped to the last page I saw and pointed to the man standing with his hand on Langston's shoulder.

"He—or I should say Langston and his man of the moment—felt safe here. Langston knew I wasn't going out and telling anyone about his secret life. I didn't go anywhere and didn't know anyone outside of my salons."

"Oh, I see." It was true that I hadn't noticed any wearable coats for Cousin Ella to go out in during New York City's cold, snowy winters.

"Y'know, that's why Langston was so leery about your dad. Your dad would come here and stare at them. No matter what Jack thinks, I knew your dad well enough to know he wasn't shy. I just think he didn't know how to act around artists—at least, not at first. But Langston knew that Doyle could destroy him. Those were not times when men like Langston could safely tell the world who they loved."

"Dad made me embarrassed when I was fifteen. He took me to see the Jewel Box Revue at the Apollo Theatre on 125th Street."

"Yeah, we know where the Apollo is, Carrie." Jack was sipping.

"This show had vaudeville-type performers dressed as men and women. But the show posters said there were twenty-five guys and one girl. Dad dared me to guess which performer might be the woman. After I got used to the acts—all by performers who appeared to be women—I thought it was fun. I had to wait to the end of all the show for the secret to be revealed . . . when the MC, dressed in a suit and tie, let her hair down. By then, though, I don't think either of us cared about that. The gender they'd presented didn't matter. And I still can't say anything for their sexual orientation. I just knew that they were good performers and we'd enjoyed the show. I left the theater humming 'I Am What I Am.' Dad couldn't talk to me about gay people himself. So he let the show do it for him."

"Yeah. Maybe Doyle should've talked to you about that instead of taking you to that spectacle. We knew some of those boys. They meant well. But I never liked that they had to make fun of themselves to make a living."

When she put it that way, I thought Cousin Ella was right. Maybe it wasn't much different from old black-face vaudeville. I felt more embarrassed than when I was fifteen. I should have known better.

"Did Langston really think Dad would've outed him?"

"How would Langston know what Doyle would do? Doyle had lived with your prudish mother all those years. Besides, even though they were cousins, Doyle and Langston didn't know each other very well then. Langston could read people better than anyone I knew, but he didn't want to take a chance if Doyle could ruin him."

"Dad wouldn't have cared."

"Yeah, I knew that but Langston didn't know that Doyle was OK with that. Your dad worked downtown in the post office with all kinds of people. Sometimes, after work, he'd hit the bar with his Irish, West Indian, and Italian friends."

"Yeah, I remember. Some of them who were still around went to his memorial service."

I thought of the days Dad would come home around midafternoon smelling of Scotch and menthol cigarette smoke.

"After the war, Doyle was deeply pained by what happened to Jews. Before then, he used to complain about how Jews owned all the stores in Harlem. That wasn't true, of course. After all, our other cousin Lou owned a cleaner shop. But after the war, I didn't hear a peep of complaint from Doyle about whoever owned what. Anyway, more stores here had changed by then, with more black, West Indian, and Latino owners. Naw, Doyle would never out Langston. Your dad was always a sensitive guy. What he saw of suffering in the war made him even more caring."

"But he still talked about it with Romare, right?"

"No. Romare only came around here for a month or two. He had his art to do. So Doyle and Langston became my salon regulars. They had to make do with each other's company. And sure, others dropped by once in a while."

I said, "Like Katherine Dunham?"

Cousin Ella gave me an evil look.

Jack sat straight up in his seat. "Stop that, Carrie. Leave Ella alone, or you're out of here." His voice was booming. "Ella was and still is a great dancer. Only thing that stopped her was the accident."

Cousin Ella's eyes got beady as she looked him up and down. "Jack, you know it wasn't an accident."

"Let's not go there, Ella. Not now."

I was curious. "What accident?"

Cousin Ella was right next to me. I knew she heard me, but she ignored me and instead told Jack, "Carrie said she's only looking out for *me*. Only taking *me* to that residence."

"Yeah, because Doyle knew I could take care of myself."

Cousin Ella's face looked ashen as she asked him, "And what about me?"

"You? Sure. But only if you give it up, give her what she's due."

Before I could ask what was due me, I heard the workers, who were back from lunch, banging their tools downstairs. They were making progress on Zee's floor. Mixed in those sounds were thuds of cardboard boxes outside Cousin Ella's door.

CHAPTER 8

I WATCHED COUSIN ELLA walk more slowly to the door than she had in the morning. After her spat with Jack, she seemed to have lost her swagger. She had a slight limp that I hadn't noticed before. The thought of her being arthritic—especially as feisty as she was—had never crossed my mind. In my imagination, Cousin Ella was still the dancer with the exciting life dancing in clubs in Harlem and Paris—and who knew where else! I was gradually changing my image of her to what I actually saw before me—a limping ninety-five-year-old woman in a stained, flower-print housedress.

"Put those boxes over there." Cousin Ella was in the middle of the living room directing Jimmy Two-Cent.

When he brought in the boxes and put them down next to the bedroom door, I saw a large sweat spot on the back of his shirt. Spring afternoons in New York were getting hotter, and he'd carried about a dozen folded-up boxes and rolls of tape down the street and up six flights of stairs. Even with that, he followed Cousin Ella's directions quickly, then told her, "I'm ready for what's next."

Jack yelled at him across the room, "Where's mine?"

He frowned when Jimmy Two-Cent pulled a pint of whiskey from his backpack and put it on the table next to him.

"That's all you got?"

Jimmy Two-Cent said, "That's all I could buy with the money you gave me."

Jack rubbed his chin, opened the bottle, and poured a drink. Cousin Ella walked over to him and screwed the bottle shut. I wished she'd done that earlier. He was reminding me too much of Dad's drinking.

Jack moved to the edge of his seat, trying to get closer to Cousin Ella. "Now, Ella, you're not still angry at me, are you? You know I'm done with you trying to lay that guilt on me."

Cousin Ella's eyes lost expression, as if she were daydreaming. "How can I ever let it go?"

"Ella, I know you love me. I came back here to you, didn't I?" Jack was pleading.

Cousin Ella's eyes became alert. "No one said I couldn't love and hurt at the same time."

Jack said, "I'm still looking out for you. You know that."

"With that thing? You haven't rid of it since you've been here. You watched Doyle and Langston treat me like a charity case."

What thing? Whatever it was, it was probably

already in a trash bag. They seemed to forget I was there while they played out their personal cycle of love and pain. Is this what sustained their relationship? I was intrigued—and felt guilty—for listening to them. But I couldn't turn away. Bill and I never talked about our feelings. What were we afraid to say or hear? With my attention given to them, I didn't hear Angel until she sauntered up to me.

"I finished folding. What'cha want me to do now?"

Jimmy Two-Cent was already unfolding the dozen boxes and taping the bottoms. He was stacking them in whatever space he could find next to the bed. Angel touched him on the butt. He stopped his work and kissed her on the cheek.

I had no time for this. I was paying them for a job, not affection. Apparently, given her belly, they could do that very well on their own time.

"You can pack the clothes in these boxes. Men's and women's separately."

I wanted to make it easy to take only Cousin Ella's clothes to the new residence. Angel looked in my direction but not at me. Jimmy Two-Cent nodded. They started packing from the piles of clothes Angel had arranged in rows on the dry sections of the bed. While they were doing that, my next chore was to figure out what to do with all this stuff, since all of it couldn't be moved into Cousin Ella's new studio apartment. Most of it wasn't worth donating. Who would want these old clothes?

And I still had the problem of Jack. He was nodding over and snoring in his seat on the sofa, and

Cousin Ella was nodding off in the chair. I heard the front door open. The smell of Italian seasoning and the sound of Zee's humming voice entered the apartment and roused the old couple. Angel and Jimmy Two-Cent dashed out of the bedroom as if they hadn't eaten in days and followed Zee into the kitchen.

I rushed over to Cousin Ella as she was waking up.

"I saw that construction worker, Felix, give you the contact info for a mover."

She tilted her head. "And where do you think we're moving to?"

"I know where you're going—you do, too—but I have to find a place to store your things."

Cousin Ella took a deep breath. "I told you, if Jack doesn't go with me, you'll have to carry me out of here."

It occurred to me that she hadn't left the apartment in who knew how long. Years maybe? With all her friends and family gone, she only had crazy Zee and Jack to talk to. If Jack had been tippling every day, as he was doing, she probably didn't have him to talk to much either—though that could have been good if they argued all the time. By tomorrow Zee and Angel would be moved too. I imagined that for a spunky woman like Cousin Ella, her life could be very lonely. How long could she go on in her senior living apartment without Jack? I was her only living relative, and I'd be in Seattle. She'd be all alone. She couldn't last long in her new place.

"Why don't you ever go out?"

She turned her face toward me so I could see the scar. "Why do you think?"

So, she had never made peace with the scar. Her anger was like acid burning through her spirit. It narrowed her place in the world. Her salons were safe because she controlled them in her space. As she said about Langston, she too would not be outed in her own apartment. She never had to walk out of her door. Her friends, groceries, even rent money came to her. There she was, standing in front of me, looking down at her ratty pink slippers. How much she must have missed her dancing shoes! I heard the paper she was twiddling with in her pocket. She looked up at me with squinted eyes.

"Carrie, what do you expect from me? These 'things,' as you call them, are my life's history. You're tossing them out like trash. Without them, I have nothing left. And you want to take away Jack, too!"

I was beginning to feel sorry and afraid for her. I'd watch her more closely. But we both knew that the choice was already made for us. Fact: The new building owners wanted her and all the residents out the next day. Where they went was their business. Only the lucky ones could go somewhere to sleep other than a park bench.

"You see that little hat over there, the one you threw in the corner over there like junk?"

I looked at the squashed gray tam with the bent feather on the side. I nodded.

"That one was my favorite. It looked good with everything."

She bent down slowly, stretched to pick up the hat, and put it on before she turned to me with a big grin. The hat looked like a moldy pancake. The feather hooked around her ear. It might have been jaunty in its day, but now it was just pathetic with her short, frizzy widow's peak sticking out on her forehead.

I smiled. "It's cute."

She snatched it off her head, looked at it for a moment, and threw it back on top of the junk heap.

"You don't have to flatter me, Carrie. I can see. I know what I look like. That hat doesn't work anymore."

Honestly, I was losing patience with her dramatics. My own possessions were ready to be loaded onto a long-haul truck in less than twenty-four hours. I had to deal with her move, quickly.

She mumbled, "What's the use."

She quickly took the paper out of her pocket and smacked it into my hand. As I read Hector the mover's number, she said, quietly, "Be gentle with us."

"I'm keeping my promise to Dad to help you."

Cousin Ella held onto my arm as we made our way to the kitchen.

Tomato-sauce-stained paper plates, gold-rimmed dinner dishes, and a plastic soup bowl were all over the Formica counter. The large open pizza box covered the small kitchen table.

Zee was perky. She, Angel, and Jimmy Two-Cent had wolfed down most of the pizza. Jack was nibbling on a slice.

Angel pointed to the open box. "We saved those for you and Ella."

The two cold pizza slices with congealed cheese didn't look very appetizing to me, but I was hungry. I found two paper plates and gave Cousin Ella her slice.

As Angel started back to her chores in the bedroom, she turned to Zee.

"Mama, how come you're always saying that Carrie is my sister? She doesn't look nothing like me."

Zee's perkiness deflated. "Well, she shoulda been if Doyle had been honest."

Ha! This crazy woman had the nerve to call Dad dishonest?

Angel looked at me, measuring every facial feature. I couldn't eat any more cold, soggy pizza crust.

Cousin Ella put down her almost-finished slice.

"Zee, haven't we had enough of that nonsense talk about you and Doyle?"

"Look! He was the only one of all of you who had a j-o-b. I mean a real one. Everyone else I saw around here was scufflin' like a bunch of headless chickens for your next dollar."

Cousin Ella reared back in her chair. The plastic seat cover squeaked.

Zee wouldn't stop. "No offense, Ella-Honey, but you know yourself that before Jack showed up you woulda starved and been homeless without Doyle and Langston. Yeah, Langston had some money then. He paid your rent, didn't he? Oh yeah, and before that he even got you your ticket back to Harlem when you had to leave Paris! Jack had money but he made himself scarce. You told me that yourself."

Angel and Jimmy Two-Cent skulked out of the kitchen to get back to work in the bedroom. I felt embarrassed for Cousin Ella, but I couldn't say anything to shield her from Zee's frank assessment. I took my cue from Jack, who said nothing.

"And look at us now, Ella-Honey. We're both going to be homeless anyway. Your cousins are both dead. They can't help you."

Cousin Ella put the rest of her pizza slice back in the box and closed it.

"Zee, they are helping me right now. Both of them."

Cousin Ella turned her head toward me. I knew that Dad was helping her through me. But Langston?

Zee paused to think about that. I saw Angel and Jimmy Two-Cent tiptoe back around the kitchen door to eavesdrop.

"Ella, you must be seeing spooks. The only person I see to help is Miss Carrie and she thinks she's too good to eat our pizza. She sure coulda helped more by giving it to me and not wasting good food."

Cousin Ella was getting her spunk back. "Zee, you've got your own business to mind. Your door is already busted down. What are you and that knocked-up daughter of yours going to do in the morning?"

Jimmy Two-Cent said, "What? What did you say about my baby?"

He couldn't say another word before Zee stood up and yelled at Cousin Ella.

"Don't you talk about my Angel that way! That college boy wants to marry her and have a good life. Better than mine, that's for sure!"

Jimmy Two-Cent put his arm around Angel's shoulder. Angel looked up at him and smiled.

Cousin Ella looked straight in Zee's face.

"That college boy doesn't have a job. All of you will be homeless together."

Zee's brown face turned brick red.

"At least he'll marry her. You and Jack never did, did you?"

Cousin Ella said slowly, "We had our reasons not to."

"None of you artsy people got married, now that I think of it. Doyle was the only one—and he wasn't really one of you. He came around later."

"He was family. He was one of us."

Cousin Ella seemed wistful. I sensed she was trying not to cry.

Zee persisted. "Not really. He had a job and little Miss Carrie. He was trying to keep a roof over her head after Janie . . . he didn't hang on in here like he had nowhere to go, like some of those *ar-teests* who came to your salons."

Zee looked at me. It hurt me to hear how she said my mother's name. The crash happened when I hit puberty—just when I needed Mom most. But over the years my grief for her was well worn. Sure, it hurt and I missed her terribly, but it was not as close to the surface as how I felt the fresh pain of Dad's passing.

Zee was a relentless motormouth. "And that Langston . . . he was homeless, too, you know."

"Zee, that's enough! You don't know."

"He sailed around the ocean blue doing who knows what on merchant ships, with no pot of his own to piss in!"

"Zee!" Jack's voice boomed in from the living room.

Cousin Ella shouted. "It's OK, Jack. Zee was just getting ready to leave."

Zee put her hands on her hips. "M'dear Ella-Honey, Zee is not ready to leave just yet! It's bad enough that the new building owners are kicking us out. But you, too? I know I can spend a few more hours with you if I want. I'm gonna help Angel. Maybe Miss Carrie might see her way to giving us a little more pay."

Zee strolled into the bedroom. Cousin Ella rushed up behind her.

"Zee! This is still my apartment. I didn't invite you into my bedroom!"

I did a quick calculation of how much cash I had. I had enough to pay her for the next hour before I'd have to leave to go to the lawyer. I thought that I could go there for an hour or two, then come back here.

"Cousin Ella, let her help. We need to get this done."

"You're gonna pay me, right Miss Carrie?"

I nodded.

Cousin Ella was downcast. She shook her head and whispered, "So this is really happening?"

I didn't know if Cousin Ella was talking to me or to herself.

If Jack's eyes had been arrows, I'd have been squirming on the floor in a puddle of my own blood. But old man Jack didn't intimidate me. In his seat, he firmly crossed his arms, spread his legs out, and positioned himself so he could watch inside part of the bedroom.

Angel, Jimmy Two-Cent, and now Zee were piling up boxes outside the bedroom door. I had to call Hector, the part-time mover. The bathroom was the only private place I could find to make the call. The brass doorknob almost fell off when I twisted it. When I finally got the door open, I understood immediately why it had been tightly shut. The stench was an assault on all my senses. I could taste it. I touched the sink, encrusted in rust and filth, to try to get water to flow. The faucet didn't work. The toilet wouldn't flush. The mirror on the medicine cabinet was in broken shards. I ran out into the living room where the mask of rose perfume was welcome. Cousin Ella had heard me jiggling the doorknob and turned her face in shame when she saw me emerge from that sewer of a bathroom. I went into the kitchen, where the water was still dripping in the sink, to wash my hands.

The hallway, with its milder stink, was the only option. I went out there and sat on the stairs. The old marble was cold on my butt. I heard the cracking sounds of a door being knocked off its hinges by the construction workers on the floor below. The squatters' voices were an unintelligible, loud mixture of tears, anger, and resignation that echoed in the stairwell. I heard Felix's Spanish-accented voice. He sounded apologetic. He said he was just doing his job. Tomorrow he'd be at Cousin Ella's door. I could not let her be humiliated by having her door crashed in.

I called the number on the crumpled paper.

"Hector? This is Carrie Stevens. Felix gave me your—Oh, he told you? . . . You're on your day job? Well, how soon can you help us move? . . . Tomorrow, yes . . . when is your shift over? . . . Two? . . . OK . . . so you can be here by 2:30?"

I thought if he could get her boxes and furniture out by four, that would give me time to get to the airport for the red-eye.

"I don't know where the stuff's going. I mean, I don't know yet . . . Yes, of course I'll know tomorrow! . . . See you then."

Felix saw me on the stairs.

"How is *abuelita*?"

"OK. Felix, can you wait until Hector comes before you break down her door tomorrow?"

"I can try to stall the guys. Just don't be too late. Abuelita is a dignified lady, isn't she?"

"Yes, she is."

"You got that right!"

Cousin Ella? I turned around and Cousin Ella was in her doorway listening to us. Felix bowed his head to her and started to go back downstairs.

Just as I stood to go into the apartment, Zee bolted out of the door and almost pushed Cousin Ella down the staircase. Felix jumped up and caught Zee while Jack was lumbering behind without his cane.

"She got the ring! She got the ring!" Jack's yelling echoed in the stairwell.

A few young squatters hung over the downstairs rail and looked up, then disappeared. Zee shook loose from Felix and disappeared too.

Felix and I helped Cousin Ella back into her apartment and into the armchair. Angel and Jimmy Two-Cent were hiding out like scared sheep in the kitchen.

Jack was holding onto the railing in the stairwell. He couldn't move. I saw his cane next to the sofa, brought it to him, and helped him limp in the door and onto the sofa. He was panting and stretched out on his back over the three sofa seats.

Angel and Jimmy Two-Cent came over to tend to him. I went to help Cousin Ella. Felix was backing out of the door.

"I have to get back to work. I hope Abuelita will be OK."

Cousin Ella nodded toward him. "Thank you."

Then she looked at Jack sprawled on the sofa.

"What happened, Jack?"

His breathing was more regular.

"I saw her put your ring—the one I gave you—in her pocket."

"What about them?"

Cousin Ella pointed to Angel and Jimmy Two-Cent.

"Them? They didn't know what was going on. They were working. They're OK."

Angel said, "That's right. We were too busy and didn't even know she was in that room."

Angel looked toward the bedroom. She was putting distance between herself and her mother.

Jimmy Two-Cent helped Jack ease up to sitting.

Jack picked up the pint bottle of whiskey, poured a drink. "I tried to get it back, but Zee pushed me and ran out. You saw her!"

As Cousin Ella watched him sip, her face tightened and the wrinkles on her forehead deepened.

"That was the ring that you brought to me when you got here from Paris?" Her voice was flat, expressionless.

"Yes. Remember? I thought you would like it, that it would have some meaning for you." Jack sipped again and Cousin Ella stared at a blank spot on the wall behind him.

"Yeah, I remember you told me that Langston helped you choose it."

"He went with me to shop for it on Montmartre."

Cousin Ella turned abruptly to Angel.

"Go get your mother!"

Angel twiddled the edge of her T-shirt.

"But I don't know where . . ."

"Yeah, you know where she is. Where else could she be?"

Angel didn't move.

Cousin Ella said slowly, "You don't want me to call the cops, do you?"

I had seen the cops on the sidewalk when I'd looked out the window. She had probably seen them, too. I'd suspected they were there in case any displaced tenants created a problem when they were told they had to get out.

Jack interrupted. "Ella, we can't do that. The cops will put us out now."

She told Jack, "Carrie has a phone. We can call whoever we want."

Cousin Ella was defiant. Jimmy Two-Cent was wide-eyed when Cousin Ella said "cops." Angel slinked out of the door and I felt relieved that I wouldn't have to call the cops. They might have put Cousin Ella and Jack out immediately. I didn't want to see these two old people and their possessions strewn about on the street.

I said to Jimmy Two-Cent, "You can get back to work. Zee isn't your problem. You're doing a good job."

He half smiled and glanced at the front door. Neither Angel nor Zee had returned yet.

"Miss Carrie, we're almost finished in here. I'll go get more boxes for the stuff in the living room."

He was edging toward the door. I nodded, yes, to let him go.

"How are you both?" I was concerned that this was too much excitement.

Jack leaned forward and put his hand on his back.

"I bumped myself on the door knob, but I've had a few aches and pains in my life that were worse."

Cousin Ella snapped back, "Yours weren't as bad as one of mine."

I'd heard that old people sometimes got into a "my ache is worse than yours" competition. But Cousin

Ella's forceful demeanor said this was something else. This was not what I wanted to listen to right now, and I really didn't want to take either of them to any emergency hospital visits today.

"So, Cousin Ella, you look OK." I tried to be upbeat, but I really felt I was sinking into a world I couldn't file into a neat category.

"Yeah, I'm OK. But, Jack, I remember that Langston said he loaned you the money for that ring and I know you never repaid him." She was businesslike, in the way I often talked to Bill.

"He never asked for it."

"You had the money. You were taking advantage of family ties. You knew very well that he wanted to feel connected, like he was family. But you were the outsider. Not Langston!" Her voice was rising but controlled, with no anger.

"He never treated me that way. Neither did Doyle. I had just lost my club. I was down and out, but I wanted to show you I loved you even though there was a wall between us. Langston knew that, so he helped me."

I heard a barely perceptible slur in his speech.

"You were never down and out, at least not then."

No one heard Angel and Zee enter the living room. They were standing behind me. Cousin Ella noticed them first.

"Well, well, well. Here's the thief herself!"

"Ella-Honey, I'm so sorry. I don't know why I . . ."

Zee was tearful. Angel was standing next to her silently.

Jack made his hands into fists. I was afraid that he'd try to hit Zee. If he did, I didn't know who would be hurt most, his hand or her face.

"Where's the ring, Zee?"

Zee took it out of her pocket and looked at both Jack and Cousin Ella. She didn't seem to know who to give it to.

Cousin Ella snatched it and held it out to examine it under the lamp. I walked over to take a look. It was a diamond—maybe half a carat—on a gold band.

Jack, still on the sofa, slid closer to the table where she was standing.

"I gave that to you as a token of sorrow for what had happened that night. I wanted your forgiveness."

With her back to him, she said, "I never wore it. I didn't want to wear your guilt."

Zee, Angel, Jimmy Two-Cent, and I were silent. Jack stared at Cousin Ella. His lips were quivering.

"Don't say that, Ella. It hurts, really bad. I wanted to make it up to you."

Cousin Ella turned to him and pointed to her scar.

"Not as much hurt as I've felt. How could you ever make up for this and what it did to me?"

Jack teared up.

"I did my best for forty-some years being here with you."

"You never even repaid Langston."

She stared at Langston's photo on the wall as if he were talking to her, and she quickly turned to face Zee. She opened her hand with the ring.

"Here. Take it. It will help you pay for a room somewhere until you get on your feet."

Zee looked confused.

"Take it, Zee! I don't need it where I'm going."

"Ella, Ella! What are you doing?" Jack was whining and crying at the same time.

Zee just looked dumbfounded and wouldn't take the ring. Cousin Ella walked over to Zee and forced the ring into her hand.

I couldn't believe that she was giving away a diamond—especially now, when she needed it herself.

Zee cried and hugged Cousin Ella.

Angel came over to look at the ring. "That's a real diamond, isn't it?"

Jack regained his posture. "Do you think I'd give her a fake?"

Angel looked at the rhinestone ring on her left hand and looked up at Jimmy Two-Cent.

Jack skulked off to the window.

When Zee tried to hug Cousin Ella again, Cousin Ella backed off. Zee looked puzzled and left with the ring.

CHAPTER 9

✦

AFTER THE BUSINESS with the ring, my mind felt like a scrambled to-do list. I tried to sort it out by putting "pack," "move," "sign in to assisted living" on Cousin Ella's side of my mental ledger. That would fulfill my promise to Dad. But my loyalty to Bill meant that something would have to be cut short for Cousin Ella. Could I throw away more of her possessions—her history, as she called them? Probably not. Too many of her first-edition books, statuettes, paintings, and much of everything else besides old clothes had too much market value.

All I knew was that I had an hour and a half to get to the lawyer to sign my condo transfer documents and get the check from the new owner. That check would go straight into the mortgage payments for the Seattle house, though Bill could easily make the payments until I got a job and beyond that. We always split things fifty-fifty, even when his salary was higher than mine, and I had to catch up with what he put out for down payment on the house. If I got to the lawyer too late and the new owners pulled out of the deal, I'd have to wait for a new buyer before I could pay my share. Bill would show that as a loan to me on his household spreadsheet until I could pay him back.

With Angel and Jimmy Two-Cent finishing the work in the bedroom, and Jack trying to hold Cousin Ella's hand in the living room—she moved away whenever he tried—the only place I could go for a moment to think was the kitchen. Zee saw me and pointed to the bedroom.

"You want to help?" I asked Zee.

She nodded, with a look of desperation and need. I was surprised that she wasn't talking.

"OK, go ahead," I said, "but no more nonsense."

When I sat on the cracked plastic chair, it occurred to me that I had a mild headache and was sweaty. My hair was sticky and matted at the back of my neck. My jeans were dusty. For the past few hours, I'd been so focused on everything and everyone else that I hadn't felt my own discomfort.

I looked out at the wall in the living room with Langston's large smiling photo. How could he look so happy? His life wasn't always charmed. When he was a young man figuring out his life, he worked on ships that took him around the world. Being here, packing lives into boxes—knowing I'd done the same with my own—was making me anxious. The idea of running away like Langston did couldn't help me now. I was moving, but not by choice. I was supporting Bill's new life. I was happy for him. But me? How would I unpack my own life?

Before I married, yes, Dad supported me financially so that I could learn to support myself. Of course that was fine. But as I heard more and more about how he came to Cousin Ella's salons, I wondered if his just having a job in the post office was enough for him. And what would be enough for me?

"Miss Carrie, Miss Carrie! Look what I found."

Angel was holding up to my face a small black case with metal fittings on the corners.

"What is it?"

She placed the case on the kitchen table and unlatched it with both hands.

"Ta-da!"

Any expectation I might have had of hidden treasure was dispelled when I saw a jumble of old, dried-up cosmetics. What used to be creamy dark brown foundation, slightly darker than Cousin Ella, and satiny blue eyeshadow now looked like adobe bricks in little jars. Some of it had dead mold caked on top. A small mirror was shining through the mess.

Angel was excited.

"I'm going to take a few minutes off. I want to try these. I always wanted to look like a star!"

"Angel, no! The baby!" I didn't want her to get sick from the mold. But I was too late. Angel had already run off to the bedroom, probably to try transforming herself into a semblance of a pregnant Whitney Houston.

I heard Zee in there, too.

"I found a headwrap! Let me use some of that makeup. Baker thought she was looking good? She didn't see me!"

Were they fighting over moldy makeup? I didn't really want to know. I had to figure out where to store all those packed boxes and furniture. If they used up that makeup, the good thing would be that there'd be one less box to deal with.

Cousin Ella and Jack, finally, were beginning to calm down. I saw her whisper something to Jack. Then she too went into the bedroom. I didn't hear any voices in there, just a faint rustling of fabrics.

An unused-looking yellow pages was on top of the refrigerator under the pizza box. I did a quick assessment of how much funding Dad had left in his will for Cousin Ella's future maintenance and how much storage space would cost. I didn't think there would be enough for more than a month of storage. Maybe I could sell some of the most valuable items. But how could I do that within a month when I'd be thousands of miles away? Despite that, I took the directory down to search for storage services.

Before I could make a call, I heard marching footsteps coming out of the bedroom. Cousin Ella was leading Zee, Angel, and Jimmy Two-Cent in a parade into the living room. Jimmy Two-Cent wore a brown pinstriped jacket over his City College sweatshirt and a squashed tan fedora.

Each woman was wearing an ill-fitting, slightly ragged, 1950s frock. Angel kept her green T-shirt on underneath a yellow sundress. Her baby bulge poked out, straining the front row of white buttons down the middle of her belly. Her attempt at heavy makeup made her look like a rounded cartoon showgirl.

Zee put up her arms and swished her butt in a navy shirtdress with white polka dots. A bent fedora was tilted to the side of her head. Her bright red lipstick exaggerated her mouth and dark blue eyeshadow made her naturally small eyes look like pinholes.

Cousin Ella, who wore no makeup, was in a fancier black swing dress with a beaded scoop neck and full skirt with layers of fluffy fabric. She must have enjoyed that cocktail look at many Parisian parties, but now the dress hung on her as it would a scarecrow. She'd lost her limp. She was strutting.

Jack, who seemed to live in his navy pinstriped jacket, was sitting on the edge of the sofa and laughing heartily.

I wasn't. This was madness. I wanted to regain some control.

"What are you doing?"

Zee stopped her little dance. Angel stopped giggling.

Cousin Ella said, "Carrie, welcome to our salon. We want to show you what it was like when Langston and Doyle were here."

"What?"

"Miss Carrie, now I know you're not hard of hearing." Angel was adjusting the sundress over her belly.

Cousin Ella pointed to Langston's photo. "Carrie, take that off the wall and give it to Jack."

I carefully lifted the photo off the wall hooks and gave it to Jack. Cousin Ella went to the credenza and pulled out a photo of Dad. She sat next to Jack on the sofa. They both held the photos.

Zee went to put "Mr. Bojangles" on the record player.

Jimmy Two-Cent asked, "Who's that singing? I thought Bob Dylan sang that."

Cousin Ella stared at him, while Jack blurted out, "Young man, please don't mention that Dylan person here. Don't you know Sammy Davis? In my humble opinion, he was the greatest performer who ever lived."

Jimmy Two-Cent leaned back and tried to disappear into the chair cushion. I heard him mumbling, "Dylan is good too."

Zee had a big smile and tipped her hat.

"I'm Zora Neale Hurston."

Cousin Ella was quick. "No, you're not. You know she never came here."

I couldn't deal with this.

"What the hell are we doing?"

Cousin Ella looked stern.

"Carrie, I don't care who you think you are, we don't talk that way here! Look, you're playing me. You go over there and get that camera. I think it's got some film in it. This is our last salon. We need pictures."

Somehow I didn't think any of them would want to see how they looked recorded in photos, but I got the

Nikon off the bookshelf. I couldn't imagine that the film was still good. It seemed pointless to protest.

"Your Dad got me that camera, Carrie."

"Why?" I couldn't believe this. Dad never got me a camera, paid for dance lessons, or anything that he said would "distract me from my studies."

"Why? Because he knew I couldn't dance anymore. I never could write or draw. Doyle knew I needed something to keep me busy—especially since I didn't go out either. So, he thought I could learn to use that camera. I did, but I never got too creative with it, though. I just took snapshots. So get it!"

"Wait a minute! You're really saying you have this because you couldn't dance?"

I tried to get my mind around the fact that he got Cousin Ella a good camera as a consolation prize.

Zee started bobbing in her seat.

"Whoa! Look at Miss Carrie get angry."

Cousin Ella cut her eyes at Zee.

"You, shut up, Zee! Carrie, what's your problem?"

"We've got to get packed and out of this place, and you're doing some crazy playacting!"

"I don't think that's your problem, Carrie."

"You're right. It's your problem."

"You know what I think is bugging you?"

Cousin Ella was really pushing my buttons.

"What? You mean, besides what I said?"

"It's that camera, isn't it?"

I didn't answer.

"Yeah. I thought so."

All eyes were on me. I was beginning to feel panicked.

"Why did Dad give you a camera when he told me he wouldn't even pay for my dance lessons? He told me to study balance sheets!"

Cousin Ella covered her face with Dad's photo.

"Carrie, I wanted you to be self-sufficient. You had to be able to take care of yourself. Look at Cousin Ella, the woman hiding behind the mask. She would've starved without me. Isn't that right, Langston?"

Jack put Langston's photo in front of his face.

"Yeah, Doyle. And she wouldn't have been able to pay her rent without me—though that guy Jack helped out when he could."

Angel, Zee, and Jimmy Two-Cent were sitting quietly, watching Jack and Cousin Ella. They turned to me to see if I'd respond. I didn't.

"Langston, you know that Carrie had talent. That dancer even told you."

I couldn't restrain myself.

"Who told you?"

Langston-Jack said flatly, "Tyree. Tyree said you would have been a great lead. But in the end, he understood why you opted to stay in college."

I felt like I might have a panic attack.

"What are you talking about? You all knew Tyree Jones?"

Dad-Cousin-Ella went on.

"You know very well that it wouldn't have worked for her after what happened to that dance group."

It was hard for me to admit that, a few years after I'd auditioned, I'd heard it was having financial problems, maybe going bankrupt. I was in denial about that. I wanted to hold onto the time I experienced my dream of dancing success, when I could've been Tyree's lead.

"Yeah, but Doyle, there could have been others. That girl had spunk. She'd have auditioned until she got something else."

"And in between her dance jobs, I'd still be supporting her because I knew too well that Bill never would have married her."

"But I might have found other ways to support myself between dancing. I wouldn't have needed Dad or Bill."

They went on.

"Doyle, did you ever think of what you would have done if she ignored you—you know, did what she wanted?"

"Carrie? Never."

Dad-Cousin-Ella laughed behind the photo. "No, not Carrie. She knew how hard I worked to keep her fed and clothed. No. Carrie was a loyal girl. A loyal woman now. She never would have gone off to be a dancer. She knew I was right."

I mumbled, "Why wouldn't I? I could have chosen not to be 'loyal' to your wishes. But why didn't I?"

Dad-Cousin-Ella looked toward me.

"Because I trained you to be loyal."

Langston-Jack sipped a drink under the photo and continued.

"I went off to be a writer, Doyle. I worked hard at it—had my ups and downs. But I've done pretty well at it, wouldn't you say?"

"Langston, but you don't have a clue. You don't know what it is to have a child—a daughter who you try to protect and who you want to be able to survive and flourish."

"Dad, did you really want me to flourish, or just survive?"

Dad survived war, Mom's death, raising me. Yes, he taught me how to survive. I'd done that well with Bill. But I was beginning to realize that maybe Dad didn't know how to teach me to flourish. I'd have to teach myself.

Langston-Jack was quiet for a moment, then continued talking to Dad-Cousin-Ella.

"No. I don't know that. I didn't get along that well with my own father, so I don't really know how to be a good son myself, much less have one."

"Yeah, Langston, look at you. I would have given anything to have a father who'd send me to college—Columbia, no less. I would've worked hard. I could've had a better life!"

"Maybe. But I don't think I would've," Langston-Jack said. "How could I live with a father who had problems with himself, who he was . . . that he was black? How could I ever accept myself and others if I had stayed with a man so narrow-minded?"

"I would have gone to that college, then found my own way." Dad-Cousin-Ella's voice was clear. But I wondered if Dad would've really found his own way. Would he have taken that risk?

Langston-Jack laughed.

"Doyle, Doyle! How do you know that? Are you really that much of a hypocrite that you'd do that for yourself but you wouldn't let Carrie do the same? What if she wanted to 'find her own way'?"

The Nikon slipped out of my hands. When it landed on the carpet, the lens cap popped off. Cousin Ella lowered Dad's photo. Jimmy Two-Cent picked up the camera. I had been too distracted to use it.

He inspected it and held it toward Cousin Ella. "The camera's OK."

He offered me his seat and sat next to me on the chair arm. He put his hand on my shoulder. I didn't move his hand away. Angel looked annoyed.

In the momentary silence, I heard Sammy Davis sing, "They said I dance now at every chance and honky tonks / for drinks and tips."

Langston-Jack took another sip from his drink, covered his face with the photo, and continued.

"I had to get away, go to sea. I couldn't be what my father wanted from me. I had to see other cultures, other people."

Cousin Ella looked at me.

"It's around this time when Doyle would start drinking. He didn't just take sips like Jack's been doing. He'd take a few shot glasses of Scotch."

Jack motioned to Zee to go into the kitchen.

"Get a glass."

Zee handed him a juice glass that he filled halfway with whiskey. He offered it to me. I hated hard liquor. The most I'd drink would be a little Chardonnay with dinner, maybe once a week. Whatever drink I'd have, it surely wouldn't be in the afternoon. I was feeling keyed up, though. I took a sip. It burned my throat, then the warmth spread through my gut. That sip was enough. I wasn't like Dad—at least, what I knew of him.

I gave the glass back to Jack. He and Cousin Ella covered their faces again with the photos. The music had stopped.

Dad-Cousin-Ella began.

"I know you heard me talking to Romare. You were over there by the window taking notes. I wouldn't be surprised if some of my stories show up in your books."

"I don't need to steal your stories."

"Semple? That fiction story character of yours? He couldn't handle some of the real things I've seen because you couldn't imagine them. You know I told you how Dachau keeps me awake. Well, this gets me drinking. There were these mercenaries. I don't know where they were from—maybe somewhere in northern Africa, where they speak French. They took this man, whimpering and sobbing, out to an opening in the woods. And quick as nothing they sliced off his head. Do you know what it's like to see a head with its last contorted look of pain and fear? Then see his body in a lake of blood? I see that, Langston, every day when I try to sleep after my shift."

Jack gulped some whiskey.

My stomach churned. I knew Dad was hurt, but for the first time, I was feeling his pain—as secondhand as it was. I wished that he were alive. I was overwhelmed by wanting to tell him I loved him. I hadn't said that since the audition. Now I so much wished I had told him that every day.

Langston-Jack asked, "So that's why you drink during the day?"

"Yeah, that's right. I've got to hold it together for Carrie. Without my daughter, I'd fall apart. She's my reason for living. I want her to survive because I've seen too many men and women who didn't. Even Janie . . ."

I was breathing fast—maybe too fast. I felt light-headed.

"Stop, please, stop!"

Angel said slowly, "Shit, Miss Carrie, your daddy was messed up. Now I know he couldn't have been mine."

Cousin Ella glared at Angel.

"Sorry, Miss Ella. I didn't mean to say that."

Zee spoke up. "Yeah, Ella-Honey. I thought this would be fun. You know, like those salons you used to have back in the day."

When Cousin Ella and Jack covered their faces again with the photos, I felt too weak to leave the room. I wanted to escape but my legs wouldn't move.

Langston-Jack moved closer to Cousin Ella.

"Doyle, my dear cousin, Doyle, we have all suffered."

Jack and Cousin Ella put down the photos. Jack hugged Cousin Ella. She hid her face in Jack's shoulder. I heard her sobbing.

Zee and Angel got up to hug and comfort her. Jack moved away from them and crossed his arms.

Jimmy Two-Cent looked at me and took Angel's seat. He sat staring at the three women. He asked me, "Are you OK?"

I said, "Yes," but I was numb. I saw the clock. I had exactly eight minutes to leave for the lawyer, but I felt wobbly. I couldn't walk to the door, not now. I had to find a way to relieve this new pain I felt and make this move work for Cousin Ella and Jack. Yes, I understood that it had to work for both of them.

Cousin Ella stopped crying and watched as I went over to the credenza to start packing small statuettes. When I picked up old newspapers to wrap the items, I saw *Constructive Anatomy*, an old red book with frayed binding. Dad's signature was on the first page.

Cousin Ella pulled away from Zee and Angel. The mother and daughter went into the bedroom.

"That was your dad's art book. He used that to learn how to draw people."

Her voice was still shaky.

The book's glossy pages were aged brown and snapped at the binding when I carefully turned them. They wouldn't hold together for much longer. These were pages my father touched. When I touched them I felt a chill of sacred connection to him. The illustrations showed bones and muscles, and a series of sketches from blocks to rounded forms. The final drawing in each section resembled a strong, muscled, male body part. Except for a few female heads, all of the drawings were of men. None of the drawings formed together to resemble a full human figure. I wondered how Dad learned to draw women.

Cousin Ella was pointing to the stack of papers in front of me.

"Do you see the black leather folder underneath?"

I dug under the papers and found it. I glided my fingers over the leather. It was scratched but smooth.

"Doyle called that his portfolio."

I had never seen Dad with this. He must've hidden it from me. I was eager to open the string ties.

Dad had torn many pages from spiral drawing pads. On the top was a study of female form. Its face appeared to be a young Zee, but its body, though female, had muscles like the men in the red drawing book. It was not provocative. It was simply the typical seated nude that would be expected in any art student's practice.

Cousin Ella was quick to say, "He never touched her. He paid her to sit. She always needed money."

Zee popped her head out from the bedroom.

"Ella-Honey, you know he liked me!"

Cousin Ella laughed and watched me turn the pages.

He did many of these studies of Zee from different angles. They were competent drawings, but not of the quality I saw in the paintings on the living room wall. Other drawings were under a piece of cardboard beneath them. The paper of those was better quality and had straight, not torn, edges. Two drawings were of my mother. He did them from a portrait photo we all loved. He emphasized in the shading the quiet spirit in her soft dark eyes, her gentle smile.

I was surprised to see the next one. It was a spirited drawing of me from around the time of the dance audition. I looked determined, almost fierce. My eyes were looking straight ahead. My mouth was clearly speaking, saying what, I'll never know. My jawline was firm, not soft like my mother's. I took a few minutes to examine this former self. Who was that talented young woman so full of confidence and determination? Is that what Dad saw in me then? Is there any of that still in me? That young me filled me with awe.

Cousin Ella gently touched my arm.

"Doyle loved you both . . . dearly."

I felt overwhelmed. So many competing emotions were coursing through me. Resentment about not being a dancer. Impatience with prepping for moving, Cousin Ella's and my own. Annoyance with Zee, and Angel's occasional impertinence. So much else I couldn't pinpoint. Despite that, I had to admit to myself—as hard as it was—that by sending me to Cousin Ella, Dad was showing me a way to see him and myself differently. Sure, it was his way, and he had his contradictions and failings. That didn't matter. He loved me and the people in this apartment. I had no idea what to do with these feelings.

I took Cousin Ella's frail hand. When I squeezed it, she quickly let go as Zee and Angel strolled into the middle of the living room. They still had on those old clothes and garish makeup. Zee stepped up to Jack like some seductive caricature, with Lena Horne's lilting voice.

"Hey, we need a break. I thought we were gonna have some fun with that salon. You know, like the good old days!"

Angel stepped up to him. "Yeah. You guys made it a real downer."

I couldn't believe it. Another break? After the pizza and "salon"? "No. We need to get this work done."

They ignored me. Jack was already up and putting on a record. A Lindy hop. He turned it up so loud that the speakers on the record player sounded tinny. It didn't matter. The jumping beat had an effect on all of us. Our bodies moved.

Jimmy Two-Cent came out of the bedroom and started his hip-hop version of a Lindy with Angel. Jack leaned on Cousin Ella, and though they were a little slow, they managed to do some good twists and swings. Zee came over to me.

"We used to dance like this with Langston. He said he felt good seeing us happy. Let me show you how we did it."

Before I could answer, Zee had taken my hand and was leading me around to the fast beat. I quickly caught on and started leading her. My heart was beating faster. We all kept bumping into each other in that small space and getting our shoes caught in the carpet. That didn't matter.

We were toppling boxes, kicking into messes the neat piles of clothes that fell out. Cousin Ella danced into a table and I saw that she got a bruise on her forearm. She didn't notice. Until I almost tripped, I didn't notice that my sneaker laces had come undone. We were all dancing to whatever beat we could keep up with. We were all spinning around the room, hopping, laughing, giggling, and panting, catching our breath. I was having more fun than I'd had in years. I felt sweaty and free.

As did many old records, this one ended abruptly. We all stood still where we were and turned toward the door. Someone was banging loudly.

With her usual calmness, Cousin Ella walked casually to the door and latched the chain lock. When she cracked it open, I saw Bill's chin jutting inside.

CHAPTER 10

✦

"I'M HERE TO SEE Carrie Stevens."

Bill's TV announcer voice, sounding like he was holding his breath to avoid the smells, came through the crack in the door.

I was still panting. I tried to whisk the dust off my jeans. If he wanted to go with me to the lawyer's office, the least I could do was look clean. I doubted, though, that he'd want to be seen with me at all, as sweaty and dusty as I was. And I was in jeans, not proper business attire for the appointment.

"You're Bill?"

"Cousin Ella, yes, he's my husband. You can let him in."

"Yeah, I know. Doyle told me about Bill years ago." Cousin Ella hesitated for a few moments, then unlatched the chain lock.

There he was in his white shirt, blue tie, tan blazer, and navy slacks. Bill was quite handsome. When we'd walk down the street, he'd gloat when beautiful women would mistake him for a movie star like Denzel. I saw Angel gawking at him.

He took one step inside the living room and said, loudly, "What the hell!"

Angel's face shifted to an intense frown. She looked to Cousin Ella, who didn't respond to his language.

Instead, Jack was grinning. He was alert, ready to tangle. He lifted his glass to Bill.

"Come in, son. Would you like a drink?"

Bill shook his head and said, "No, thank you." Then he added, "Isn't it a little too early for that?"

Jack kept smiling.

"No, son. It's my glass and my whiskey. And this is where I live. I'll drink whenever I want to."

For the first time in the almost twenty years that I'd known him, Bill had nothing to say. He looked stunned that the old man would challenge him. He stood across from me in the living room, tightly grasping his polished black attaché case.

He repeated in a whisper, "What the hell."

Cousin Ella's body stiffened.

"If you say that again, you can leave! Carrie, I thought you married a gentleman. That's what Doyle told us."

Bill furrowed his brow and looked at her as if she were a quaint humanoid specimen. For a moment, I saw him eye Cousin Ella's scar, then he scanned the room.

"Bill, meet my family. Cousin Ella and Jack. And these are their friends, Angel, Jimmy Two-Cent, and Zee."

I smiled politely and tried to be cordial, but Bill had no pleasantries to offer.

Bill scrutinized each one's shabby vintage clothes and clownlike makeup as I pointed to them and said their names. Bill often called unusual people "circus acts." To Bill, their bizarre appearances must have quite outdone anything Barnum and Bailey could have dreamt up.

Everyone mumbled "Pleased to meet you" in a way that sounded like the Tower of Babel.

Bill could barely say hello to them while he focused on me with deadly precision.

"Carrie, is there somewhere we could go to talk . . . privately?"

Zee blurted out, "You're not very friendly, are you?"

He looked at her matted hair and smirked.

"Sorry, I'm in kind of a rush. Wouldn't you say, Carrie?"

He made me feel awkward by putting me on the spot like that.

Cousin Ella said, while extending a welcoming palm toward the bedroom, "You can go in there. We have a lot to do out here."

He saw the knocked-over boxes and strewn clothes near the bedroom door.

Bill said, "Yes, I can see that."

I knew he was being what my dad would have called "nice-nasty." I couldn't let him slight these people who I had just danced and laughed with. I pointed to the remaining stacked boxes.

"We've been working at it."

Bill brushed by me as he headed toward the bedroom.

I followed him there and opened the window and the blinds. In the light, the room looked bigger than before, when it was completely cluttered with random piles of old clothes. Angel and Jimmy Two-Cent still had to finish sorting and packing the few remaining stacks on the side of the room where the red dress was still on the floor. Bill put his attaché case on top of the dresser. He sat in the damp spot on the bed. I didn't tell him to move.

Cousin Ella closed the door. Except for a little giggle from Angel and a "shush" from Zee, it was exceptionally quiet. I knew they were at the door listening.

"What is this madhouse?"

Bill started ranting. When he did this, I found it best not to try to listen or talk until he was done. This time I couldn't hold my tongue.

"Cousin Ella is my only family and they're her friends. Don't talk about them like that."

"Oh, so now I'm not your family?"

"No, that's not what I meant."

"Well, it's how you're behaving. Look at you."

He dismissively brushed his hand in the air toward my body.

"These are my blood kin. Cousin Ella is."

He looked at me as if I'd gone mad too. When he stood and paced in the small area at the foot of the bed, I saw the damp circle on the seat of his pants. He didn't seem to feel it.

"I knew you'd never make it to the lawyer's. You're too 'busy' in this insane asylum."

"Why do you keep saying that?"

"Because I just state facts as I see them. And, look at you! You look and smell almost as bad as they do."

"Why did you come here? You were too busy with your own business this morning."

He looked at me with a slight smile.

"Why do you think I'm here? I'm concerned about the condo sale. That little bundle of cash will come in handy."

I couldn't believe what he was saying. I didn't go to grad school. Instead, I worked hard so he could. I paid for the mortgage, food, and almost everything else. I didn't have much savings because of that. And he was treating that like a throwaway?

"So, as you see it, my condo in Greenwich Village—that you lived in all these years, that I worked hard to pay the mortgage when you were in grad school—will just provide a 'little bundle'? You know that it could buy that whole house in Seattle."

"Yeah, yeah. So, what?"

"No, you can't dismiss it like that!"

"I'm not dismissing it. But we could use the cash to get settled in."

"You know you have the cash."

His sly smile made his face look more masklike than handsome.

"Look, I brought a notary. She can get you to sign the papers and make them legal. We'll be done with the sale so we can move on."

"Where's the notary?"

"She's waiting down in front of the building. She didn't think she could walk up."

I looked out the window. I saw a middle-aged blond woman in khaki slacks and a blue blazer with a large tote bag jerking her head around, looking in all directions. She was stepping cautiously, trying to avoid the pipes the construction workers left on the sidewalk. A young, curly-haired woman in athletic pants with a market bag on her shoulder emerged from the renovated building next door. She walked over to the blond and started talking. I could hear their words echoing against the building in the long silence between the banging of doors downstairs.

I heard the young one. "So if you're applying for an apartment in that building, I'd suggest the top floor. That's what I have in this one. You'd get great views!"

"How's the neighborhood?"

"Ah, well. It's getting better, slowly, but improving. There are a couple of nice new shops, a café or two . . ."

Bill was rustling papers in his attaché case. He stopped when I turned around.

"How am I going to sign anything if she's down there?"

"Obviously you have to go down there."

"Do you really think I'm going to sign away my condo in the middle of the street?"

"You're kidding, right? I made the effort to go to the lawyer, get the papers, find the notary, and come up to this foul-smelling junkyard apartment to help you get done what you should have done yourself! You should be eager to do it."

I heard Cousin Ella's muffled voice through the door. "Who does he think he is?"

"Bill! Your notary has to come up here."

I surprised myself. Normally I would have given in to him. I wouldn't have thought twice about it.

"No, she can't."

"OK. You get the papers from her and I'll take them to the lawyer myself. I can get there tomorrow before the flight."

"It'll be too late. We'll lose the sale."

"No problem if I lose the sale. I'll find another buyer."

"Yeah right. Overnight, magically, someone will arrive with a bag of cash! I can see how you fit in this family. You're as crazy as they are."

"You don't know them!" I yelled at Bill.

"You tell him, girl!" I heard Jack behind the door.

"And you just met them! What do you know?" Bill yelled back at me.

Then, as usual when he wanted to be in control, Bill regained his calm and said, "Maybe I'll give a little slack to your dad, though. He wasn't like these people. He was a normal guy."

"A normal guy? You didn't know him either!"

"Carrie, do you think you're the only one who misses him?"

After he said that, I realized that when I arrived I had only a memory of a photo of Cousin Ella in that red dress that was wrinkled up on the floor. Now I knew more about the woman who went from the cabaret dancer to this old lady in a housedress. But it wasn't only her who I knew better. I wished that I had known as much about Dad and Langston as I had learned this morning. But it was too late; they were both gone.

Suddenly, Bill walked to the bedroom door. He quickly opened it, and Cousin Ella, Jack, Zee, Angel, and Jimmy Two-Cent, who were clustered around the frame, looked sheepish.

Bill simply said, "Excuse me," and rushed to the front door and down the stairs.

Cousin Ella said, "Don't let him bully you, Carrie."

I opened the window and looked out. The notary was talking to the young woman again, whose market bag was now filled.

She told the notary, "The shops are OK. If you go to 125th Street you can find just about anything you want. Yeah, living here is a good deal. Rents and condos are less expensive than downtown. Subway lines are nearby, lots of buses . . ."

She trailed off as Bill walked up to the notary. She smiled and did a double take when she saw his wet butt. He smiled back. He must have thought she was another admirer.

"Nice talking to you. I hope we'll be neighbors. You'll like it here."

She waved goodbye and disappeared into the building next door.

Bill appeared to be whispering to the notary. A few passersby quickly looked at them with suspicion, but when Bill and the notary seemed OK, went about their business. The notary took papers out of her bag and handed them to Bill. He came back into the building, leaving her again to look every which way on the street.

I sat on the dry part of the bed to wait for him. Cousin Ella had left the front door unlocked, so when he returned, he simply barged in without acknowledging anyone in the living room and came directly to me.

He held out a folder of papers in front of my eyes.

"Sign these now. She said she was willing to put her legal stamp on them downstairs."

I took the papers and put them down on the bed next to me. He handed me a pen. I put that down.

"Aren't you going to sign them?"

"Not yet."

"Carrie, I'm trying to do what's best for us."

"I know. You always do. I appreciate that, but the condo is mine."

I couldn't believe I said that.

He stared at me, incredulous. He moved the papers to my lap and sat down next to me. He put his arm around my shoulders and kissed my cheek. That was why I loved him. His occasional moments of tenderness made tolerable what Cousin Ella suggested was his bullying. I pulled away from him. The sunlight was streaming through the blinds on his face. Yes, he was a beautiful man—exceptionally smooth brown skin, piercing dark eyes . . . I didn't want to linger on his looks too long. If he sensed I was weakening, I knew he'd use his charm to get me to sign the papers.

"Bill, did you see the paintings out there in the living room?"

"You mean those pictures on the wall. Yes. I saw that photo of Langston Hughes. You can't miss it when you come in. He was your father's cousin, right? I remember reading those stories about Semple in high school. They were fun."

"Yes, but what about the paintings? They're valuable."

"Oh, some are valuable? All I can say is keep them. Maybe we could sell them or donate them for tax deductions."

"But they're not ours."

"What can they do with them?"

"They might want to look at them."

His eyes softened.

"Carrie, whatever. Listen, the notary, she's waiting down on the street. Sign these." He poked the folder that was on my lap.

"Tell her she can leave."

"What? Did I hear right? What are you saying?"

"I'm not signing these now. I want to read what I'm signing."

"I read these already. It's simple. You sign them, we get the money."

"I'll make an appointment to go to the office and sign them with the lawyer."

Bill backed away and stood, towering over me with his muscles tensed. I flinched, then breathed myself to be calm.

"You know, Carrie, before we got married I had a talk with your father. He told me you were a smart, practical woman. He said you'd be a good helpmate, a wife who I could always depend on."

I could hear Dad saying that. At our wedding, Dad was so happy that he didn't sit down after he gave me away. He stood there beaming. My marriage to a "good provider" was Dad's payoff for what he called "raising me right." But I was beginning to wonder what would be my own payoff.

Before I'd left for Cousin Ella's, Bill had surprised me with our favorite muffins and coffee from the deli around the corner. Our last time to have that treat. At breakfast, we were surrounded by boxes that the movers had packed for us. Bill talked nonstop about his great future career designing airplanes. He expected an early promotion. I had to admit that I was impressed. But he had forgotten that I had to help Cousin Ella. When I left for Harlem, he was still drinking coffee, looking over his new job materials. I guess he took care of business later.

I finally answered him. "I have been, haven't I?"

"Yes. Sure. We've done well together. But it'll be even better when I start this new job."

"How will it be better for me?"

He went to the dresser.

"I've got more leads for you, too." He pulled a paper from his attaché case and handed it to me to skim. It was a list of managerial jobs in Seattle—all with good pay.

"You can have your pick. The people offering those jobs are in my network. Any one of them would be glad to have you work for them."

"Thank you."

"You do believe in me, don't you, Carrie? Your dad understood me. He said he liked my motivation."

"Yes, I know he did."

"I didn't have my father to go to my graduation. Your dad didn't have to do it, but he was good to me. When I graduated that year before you, he was there."

Dad had told me often how great it was that Bill was so focused on his goals. But now I wondered if Dad or Bill ever thought I'd focus on mine. But I had to be honest with myself. Things were so muddled now with so many changes that I didn't really know what mine were.

"On the way back to the condo, I'll stop at the lawyer's office to make that appointment for you. I'll call to let you know the time."

"You can't stay here to help us pack?"

"Haven't you noticed how disgusting it stinks in here? No way can I stay here. Besides, that poor woman is waiting downstairs. When will you be home?"

That "poor woman"? Did he ever notice me, how I felt? Did he always think of me as the worker bee, never the queen?

I remembered my to-do list.

"I might have to stay overnight to get everything done."

"Here? Overnight? Not only does it stink, but it's also dangerous. Did you see some of those derelicts hanging out on mattresses downstairs?"

"I'll be OK. Call me."

He paused for a second, nodded yes, and left me sitting on the bed. He didn't hug me or even kiss me goodbye. That wasn't so unusual for him, but he didn't look back either. I didn't get up to see him out.

When he left, I felt nothing, as if we were business partners. We were two people who never danced. Yes, he was a good person in his way, but the thought of moving thousands of miles for more of the same caused my chest to tighten. I started to cry.

I heard voices in the living room saying "Goodbye," but I didn't hear Bill respond.

When the door closed, I tried to regain my composure. I put the job list in the folder with the condo sale documents, and put the folder on the dresser.

I sat there thinking how Bill and I were going on twenty years of marriage. We were a good team when it came to building our investment accounts. We looked good when we went to charity events. We stayed at luxury vacation resorts, but he never held my hand. And I never held his.

Angel was standing in the doorway.

"Sorry to bother you, Miss Carrie, but can we come in now? We want to finish in here. Mom wants us to be done before night so we can get someplace in a shelter."

"Sure, come in."

She tiptoed around me. I left the room as Jimmy Two-Cent and Zee entered with their eyes down.

I was surprised to see how much they had packed in the living room while I was talking to Bill. Most of the statuettes and about half of the books were off the shelves.

Cousin Ella and Jack were on the sofa, quietly looking at the album. Cousin Ella motioned for me to sit next to her. I felt drained. It was just early afternoon, but the day was wearing on me. I didn't mind looking at photos for a few minutes.

Jack hobbled up and put on "God Bless the Child." Billie Holiday's words resonated more now than they did earlier. How long would any of us have our own? Until tomorrow?

Cousin Ella hugged me.

"You're doing good, Carrie, very good. You didn't let him intimidate you."

I didn't answer. I just wanted to see the photos on the pages she was flipping. These were large black and whites. Dad and Langston reading some papers. Dad and Langston standing and doing a toast. Dad and Langston smiling with Cousin Ella. Cousin Ella? That was the first photo I'd seen of her. She was wearing the party frock that Zee'd had on earlier. There was another man with them who looked familiar and who was taller than all of them. It wasn't Jack. He must have been the photographer for this one.

Cousin Ella pointed to that man.

"Don't you recognize Tyree?"

"Tyree? You mean Tyree Jones?"

I stared at the photo. It was an older man, but, yes, it was Tyree.

"Tyree came here? And Dad?"

"Yeah, we all knew Tyree. He was a dancer so you know I knew him."

Jack said, "She was OK with the men dancers. It was the women who bothered her. She only let Kate Dunham come here once."

Cousin Ella looked away.

"What is that? Yeow!" Angel screamed in the bedroom.

"Oh, shit! That's nasty!" Jimmy Two-Cent yelled.

Zee, Angel, and Jimmy Two-Cent came running out of the bedroom.

Zee ran at me with wild eyes.

"I told you! I told you they had bad mojo in there!"

Cousin Ella put the photo album aside and looked down at her dress.

Jack said, "They found it."

To me, this was nonsense. It was just another blip in this long day, something else I had to deal with. I went into the bedroom and looked around. I saw nothing strange.

Zee followed me. She pointed to the red dress on the floor.

"Zee, what are you showing me? You can just fold and pack it."

"Go look."

I looked. It was a red dress. So what?

"No, not there. Look underneath."

I bent down and turned the dress up. There was the doll—No! I stood up and stepped back. It was an old-style raggedy monkey doll with moth larvae crawling on it, dressed up in slightly burnt show clothes. It had a diamond-studded leather collar. It looked something like the monkey I'd seen in the photo of Cousin Ella that Dad had.

Zee pointed at that thing. "That's bad mojo! I told you it was here! I told you."

This was amusing to me. But I wondered why Cousin Ella and Jack kept such a thing hidden in their bedroom.

I went into the living room. Jack and Cousin Ella were standing. Jack was hugging her. She was loudly sobbing with her head buried into his chest.

She caught her breath and said, "Get rid of it, Carrie. Please get rid of it."

Jack yelled, "No, not yet!"

He let go of pitiful-looking Cousin Ella and hobbled into the bedroom. I and the three friends surrounded her. He came back to the living room with the collar off the doll. He held it up to me.

"They're real. It's all my profit from the club that I was able to bring back from Paris."

I moved closer. White and colored diamonds were embedded in the leather collar.

Cousin Ella said in a monotone voice, "There was a fire in his club. Table cloths, carpets, everything was going up in flames. And Jack? He ran after Mojo, his pet monkey, to save him. He couldn't, so he ripped off that collar. But you see, I was there. He left me to get burnt. He said he loved me, but he went to save that monkey."

"You know I had to get that collar." Jack softly rubbed the monkey head carved on the crook of his cane.

"That collar ruined my career. I felt like my cheek was boiling. After that I couldn't work anywhere. That collar ruined my whole life!"

"Ella, you know I tried to make amends—"

"Yeah, you did come back here to me . . . years later. And you came back here with that damned doll! You just couldn't give up that monkey!"

She said "damned"?

"Cousin Ella?"

By then, they were both crying in each other's arms. Angel, Zee, and Jimmy Two-Cent went to hide out in the kitchen.

I was shaken by what I'd heard and went back into the bedroom. I understood why she wanted to be rid of the doll. It looked like its grinning face had been bashed in. Had she done that? I picked up an old T-shirt from the garbage pile. I wanted to scoop up the monkey in the shirt, but it wasn't easy. The larvae were squirmy, and its old arms and legs tore off as I touched it. The doll was sickening, but it was more disgusting to think of what happened to Cousin Ella. I had to do this for her. Finally, I got it rolled in the T-shirt. I walked to the window and tossed the bundle out.

I watched the T-shirt open as it fell. The various body parts tore off in all directions. The grinning head hit the yellow hard hat of one of the construction workers. I heard three of them yell "Hey!," "What the hell?," and "Somebody threw a dead baby out the window!"

A young woman walking by screamed, "Call the cops!"

Windows in buildings on the street opened and concerned faces popped out.

They looked up and saw me. I yelled down, "It's a monkey doll. Only a doll."

They looked down at it. There was nothing left but cloth and dirty stuffing.

A woman's voice yelled, "You should be ashamed of yourself!"

I closed the window. The construction workers brushed the monkey doll's remains aside, out of their workspace. One guy shook the larvae off his shoes.

Cousin Ella was standing in the door watching me. She came in, took my hands, and said, "Thank you."

CHAPTER 11

✦

AFTER THE MONKEY doll incident, no one wanted to say much. We all went into our private worlds of busyness with packing. With Cousin Ella's past—traumatic and life-changing as it was—literally thrown out of the window, I thought we all needed to consider the present and deal with the harsh uncertainty of where we'd be sleeping the next night. What surprised me was that, as I quietly packed books in the living room, I was wondering that, too. I'd never liked sleeping on red-eye flights, and the thought of a one-way red-eye was beginning to seem ominous.

Angel and Zee, who were working slower, had reluctantly gone back into the bedroom to finish with the clothes and odds and ends. Jimmy Two-Cent went out for more boxes and garbage bags. When he returned, I heard him whistling in the hallway, but he was silent when I opened the door. There was no more banging and crying downstairs with doors being busted open. Those displaced squatters had left to who knows where. The construction workers' afternoon shifts were over. They'd be back in the morning.

Cousin Ella was on the sofa. She was mute, staring into space with soft eyes, and hadn't gotten up for hours. Droopy-eyed Jack was next to her on the sofa, trying to hold her hand. Sometimes she'd grab it, other times she'd whisk it away. She appeared to be meditating during the whole time it took for us to finish packing small usable and valuable items. Jimmy Two-Cent took out big bags of trash to the dumpster. Jack had finished his whiskey, and since he was monitoring her, I wasn't too concerned. His face was long and wrinkled, with no hint of a smile since she had sobbed on his chest.

I had turned my phone ringer off and noticed that Bill had called twice. I didn't return the calls or listen to his messages. I didn't want his thoughts—or commands—to clutter my mind. There was only the sound of objects moving and boxes being taped, with an occasional yell or car horn in the street. But I was slowing down, taking time to flip through the books. Many were first editions that had friendly, even loving inscriptions to Cousin Ella and Jack. I was sure that, for the old couple now holding hands on the sofa, those words were very meaningful. The more I learned of them, as best as I could, the more I began to understand the joys and sorrows of their lives. And me? Compared to them, my life had been mostly flat, with the usual ups and downs of office work, and, except for a few acquaintances, socially bereft. Sure, I was competent and productive, but . . .

I had donated Dad's things a few weeks before. I wished I'd examined each of Dad's items before I gave them away. If I'd looked at them as closely as I was Cousin Ella's, how much I would have learned. Langston, who I never knew, was still smiling there on the wall. I wanted to pack his photo last. I needed his warm and inspiring expression. He was gone decades ago; I wished I'd seen him alive. But Cousin Ella was sitting there, still breathing, still able to tell me her stories—if she would just talk.

"Miss Carrie. Miss Carrie!"

I hardly recognized my own name when Zee broke the silence. I turned from the bookshelves to see that she and Angel had changed into their own clothes. They might have tried to wipe off the stage makeup without water, but there were still red streaks of rouge on their cheeks. Jimmy Two-Cent followed them in his sweat-stained shirt.

Angel spoke quieter than before. She pointed to the stuffed garbage bags at her feet. "We're finished, Miss Carrie. All the boxes are stacked up in there. If you don't mind, we're taking some of the clothes you were throwing away."

"Yes, of course, take any you want. Take some blankets, too . . . for the baby."

Angel half smiled. I didn't want her to feel as embarrassed as she looked.

Zee reached out toward Cousin Ella but stopped short of touching her. Jack smiled weakly toward the three.

I did some quick mental numbers and went for my wallet to pay them, but they were downcast as they took the money. Zee and Angel simply stuffed it in their pockets.

Jimmy Two-Cent counted his, smiled, and said, "Yes, that's right. Thanks."

I knew he'd notice that I'd given him—in fact, all three of them—a few dollars extra. "Jimmy Green, use it for your textbooks."

He grinned and shook my hand.

They were hanging around staring at Cousin Ella. Suddenly, she had a big grin as she came out of her quiet space.

"Where are you three going?"

Zee sat in the chair facing Cousin Ella and Jack and held up a folded paper.

"I have an address of a shelter. If we can get there soon, we'll have a place to sleep tonight. But what Miss Carrie gave us might pay for a room somewhere until Two-Cent gets a job."

"Where are you going, Miss Ella?" Angel stood by her mother.

Cousin Ella said a cheerful, "To die."

Her three friends raised their eyebrows. Zee opened her mouth, but didn't speak. Jack tried to hold Cousin Ella's hand. She brushed him aside.

I winced. Yes, she was ninety-five and, yes, her next home would likely be her last. But, at that moment, she was alive and as well as she could be. Was dying all she had to look forward to?

I got three old business cards out of my purse that had my cell phone number and gave them to Zee, Angel, and Jimmy Two-Cent. "When you get phones, you can call me, if you want to know where they are."

Cousin Ella gave me a weary look. They took my cards, then took turns hugging Cousin Ella and Jack.

Angel and Zee picked up the bags of clothes, while Jimmy Two-Cent got lumpy trash bags—no doubt filled with years' worth of accumulated items—from the corner of the room to take to the dumpster.

"Well, good luck to you all," Zee shouted as she left.

Jack made an effort to wave. When the door closed, Cousin Ella looked straight at me.

"So, Carrie, where are we going? Are you going to pack us up like those books?"

"I hadn't thought of that."

"Yeah. I know that you don't know where we're going."

"The senior apartment—"

Jack sat up straight. "No. You know better than that! Look at all these boxes, and you still have more paintings to crate. There's no way in hell that all our stuff—including the furniture—will fit in that tiny place."

"The furniture?" I'd decided to leave that as junk.

Cousin Ella's face tightened.

"What do you think we're going to sit on . . . the floor?" Cousin Ella paused between words as if she were talking to a toddler. Her spunk was back.

"I think the place you're going is furnished." I remembered the model apartment I saw had basic, institutional-looking furniture.

"I want my own." She made a fist.

"I don't know if that's possible."

I looked at Jack. I still hadn't figured out what to do with him, and I think he knew it.

"Carrie, wherever you take us is OK with me," he said.

Cousin Ella sat up and glared at Jack. "No, it's not. Wherever was never good enough for you. Carrie, I need to explain something."

I sat down in the armchair. Cousin Ella was pursing her lips, but no words came out.

Finally, she said, "You know I went to Paris to dance. Soon after I got there, Bricktop said I was pretty and wanted to make me a star in her cabaret. But Jack here had his own club and was competing with her for me."

"Ella, you had charisma. Why wouldn't I want you? You brought in high-paying customers."

"Langston introduced me to Jack. I think he might have been a busboy in Jack's club for a quick minute."

Jack perked up and was feeling at the side of the sofa for the whiskey bottle. When he finally got it, he frowned because it was empty.

Cousin Ella said, "Hmmm. Well, Carrie, you're a grown married woman so I can say this. Jack had a little something that Bricktop didn't."

"Excuse me! A little something?" Jack seemed playful.

"Well, it did get bigger at times."

He grinned. Cousin Ella continued.

"We started out just seeing each other once in a while. But then, we really started to like each other."

"You mean, we loved each other."

"Yeah, Jack. We did. But you loved Mojo, too."

"Mojo? You mean that monkey?" I was confused.

"Yeah, Carrie. Jack took that monkey everywhere and controlled him as best as he could with that diamond leash. At first, I thought it was cute. Then I saw that Mojo stole food and was just the worst nuisance. Jack loved him anyway. He dressed him up in good clothes and treated him like a son."

Jack slinked back into the sofa cushion.

"He belonged to a friend of mine who'd died. Last thing I told him was my promise to keep his beloved Mojo. Then I put my savings in those diamonds on his collar. I figured I could carry that easier than cash if things got tough during the war."

I thought of how I'd made a promise to Dad's memory to care for Cousin Ella.

Cousin Ella sighed. "Well, after the fire, Jack did, at least, take me to the hospital."

"Ella, stop. Please."

"Why should I stop? This scar hasn't stopped, has it? At the hospital they just bandaged me up as if I'd just been another showgirl in a knife fight over a man. They didn't take care with fixing it to look good. So when it healed—and it looked like this—all my dancing days were over. Even Jack didn't want me in his club. He could hardly stand looking at me. Right, Jack?"

Jack was leaning over with his face in his hands.

"This was just before the war broke out really bad, and I didn't have anything. Langston didn't have much, but he pulled together enough to get me fare on a ship back here. Doyle found this place for me and paid a few months' rent to help me get on my feet. Doyle and Langston hadn't actually met each other then, but both wanted to help me."

Jack looked up.

"Ella, can't you ever forgive me? I've tried my best."

"Carrie, Jack came here to live with me years after that—long after the war."

"Ella, you know I fought in the war. I couldn't come here then. Doyle understood that."

"Yeah, he might've. But he never understood why you fought for the French."

"They gave me the chance to be a pilot. The Americans didn't think I had the right to fly."

They were quiet for a moment. I felt it would be insensitive to ask, but I did anyway. I wanted honesty because too much had been hidden from me for too long.

"Why was that Mojo doll in your bedroom?"

Ella didn't hesitate in answering.

"Because Jack still wanted to carry some semblance of that crazy monkey wherever he went. He tried to hide it from me when he moved in here. Around then, I was back to being in love with Jack. But when I saw that doll—every time I saw it—I was reminded of how that monkey ruined my life. I finally tried to deal with it. Make peace. That's when I wrapped it in that red dress because that's the dress

I was wearing that awful night of the fire. But then I had a double reminder."

I remembered seeing the torn, burnt seams on the dress.

"Ella looked good in that dress, Carrie."

I had the impression that Jack really meant she looked good "out of the dress."

"Well, now Mojo is totally gone." I was still disgusted by how it broke, with the larvae flying, when it hit the street.

Jack put his arm around Cousin Ella's shoulders. She didn't resist this time, but she was breathing hard. I was afraid she was panicking.

"Carrie, you know what Ella didn't tell you about Doyle and Langston? They did some work together."

"Dad did work with Langston?"

"Langston made little notes all over everything about writing he wanted to do. So, sometimes, he'd get Doyle to read them so that Langston could hear how it sounded. Langston would especially do this with parts in plays he was working on. He'd get Doyle to read them, sometimes we'd all help."

"That must've been fun for Dad!"

Cousin Ella regained her composure. "That's how we got to meet Tyree, remember?"

Jack said, "Ella, I didn't know you'd bring that up now."

"It's time, Jack. Now or when?"

I was curious. "Tyree and Dad? You said you knew Tyree because he was a dancer. Was there something else?"

"Yes, but it was your dad who introduced him to us. He thought Jack might like some more men at my salons. Actually, I didn't mind that either. But I learned later that Doyle had another motive."

"OK, but Dad did *what*? I don't believe that Dad knew Tyree!"

This made no sense to me. I'd always thought that Dad avoided artists like Tyree—I guess, unless he was at a salon here. How could he have known him on his own?

"Yeah, Carrie, Tyree was good to talk to and Ella liked his youthful good looks. But there was another reason."

They were quiet. Cousin Ella opened the photo album to a page she'd covered before. Cousin Ella, Dad, Langston, and Tyree appeared to be signing papers in this living room.

"OK. So, what was it?"

They looked at each other. Jack broke the silence.

"Do you think she's ready?"

"Now or never."

"Tyree is a good guy. You know that."

Of course I knew that. "Yes, he wanted me to be his lead dancer." Saying that caused a cramp in my stomach. I felt slightly nauseous.

Cousin Ella sat on the edge of her seat.

"Be glad you weren't."

Jack picked up. "Because he was never able to handle the business of that dance group. You see, Doyle read in the papers—the *Amsterdam News*—that The Tyree Jones Dance Company was having hard times. Lots of young dancers were going to lose their jobs."

"Ha! Dad was concerned about other young dancers losing their jobs? Is that why he didn't want me to have a chance?"

"Don't be so quick to judge, Carrie. All those times Doyle came here to my salons and met artists gave him a different perspective."

"Cousin Ella, OK. I'm listening."

"So we all liked Tyree and felt he was a sincere man and a great dancer."

"Yeah, so Ella, Langston, and your dad decided to help him."

What Jack had said was ludicrous to me.

"So you're saying that Dad kept me from dancing with Tyree's troupe, and then he helped him? Why?"

Jack faced me.

"That's exactly why. He knew he had made a mistake when he discouraged you. He told us that so many times we got tired of it. We were all glad when Doyle found out he could do something for Tyree."

My phone was vibrating in my pocket. This time, I couldn't ignore Bill.

"Hi. OK, 9:30. At the lawyer's . . . Yes, I'll sign them . . . No, I didn't listen to your messages yet . . . I'm busy right now. Talk to you later."

I hung up. Jack furrowed his brow.

"So, Cousin Ella, how did the three of you help him?"

"We discussed how we could back him so he could stay afloat. We pooled our funds. I sold some antiques,

Langston had a book advance, and your dad had some money saved from your mom's insurance. In return, with the three of us together, we got a high percentage of ownership in Tyree's dance company."

I sat back in the chair, trying to relax. I could never imagine Dad making such a frivolous investment.

Cousin Ella was getting excited. "We all lost at first. Your dad, who was afraid of risk anyway, was miserable. But eventually we all won in this. And that includes Tyree and his dancers. It seemed like our support motivated them. They started getting better and larger venues."

Jack fished an old whiskey bottle from underneath the sofa. It was covered in dust balls and had one shot left. He poured and sipped it.

Then he said, "Carrie, it paid off for Doyle, Langston, and Ella, too. They all used to get a little bit from it every season. But I think Langston used to put his gains back in the troupe."

"Yeah, I bet. A little."

Cousin Ella said, "Well, yes, at first it was nothing much. But I get more now because Tyree's dancers get great reviews and sell every seat when they tour the country. Another thing, rest their souls, Doyle and Langston are gone and that leaves me to get their shares. But now, since I'm not a spring chicken, I don't need that much money anymore—especially since Jack will sell those diamonds. Isn't that right, Jack?"

He paused a few seconds before he nodded. She continued.

"You know, I love Tyree's work. Someone made a video for me of his group's performance. He's a real innovator. And he's passing on his creative work to young people. I'm so happy to see that."

She pulled some folded-up papers out of her house-dress pocket and abruptly handed them to me.

"So, this is yours, Carrie. Langston's and Doyle's percentages—and a job with The Tyree Jones Dance Company. They desperately need a business manager. They've known about you for a long time and want you to do it. You have just the background they need."

"What are you saying?"

"Read it. You know how to read, don't you?"

I couldn't believe this. I was shaking and could hardly unfold the papers. One was a glowing review cut from a Chicago newspaper. Then there was the contract between James Langston Hughes, Doyle Stevens, and Ella Stevens. Down the page, my name was on it too, as beneficiary.

Cousin Ella gave me a chance to skim the contract.

Then she said, "Tyree came by here last weekend to tell us he would like to see you two days from now."

"But I'll be in Seattle."

"Hah! Ella, you said she was ready."

They both stared at me.

Cousin Ella said, "No, it's not dancing, but think about it, Carrie."

I was stunned. I heard myself whispering, "So this was my gift?"

"It's getting dark. Jack and I go to bed early on old folks' time. Tomorrow will be a busy day. We need to sleep."

I rushed into the bedroom before they could get up, turned on the overhead light, and tried to make order of the tousled, dried sheets on their bed. This would be their last night in their decades-old home. I wanted them to be comfortable. I removed the folder of papers Bill left me on the dresser and, as I smoothed the bed, I felt a lump. When I looked closer I saw Cousin Ella's ring, the one she gave to Zee. I had no way to know how it got there—if Zee dropped, forgot, or returned it. Whatever, here it was.

My mind was spinning. I wondered if I could do this work with Tyree from Seattle. Bill would be convinced of my insanity to give up, for this, all the good-paying corporate jobs that he had arranged for me. Yes, he'd think I was crazy to take on something so risky.

I brought the folder and the ring into the living room, where Cousin Ella and Jack were both cuddled and dozing off on the sofa. Cousin Ella roused when she heard my footsteps.

"Look what I found."

I held up the ring. It took a few seconds for her to focus on it.

"I gave that to Zee . . ."

Jack opened his eyes, and when he saw it, he took it very gently from me.

"Ella, it came back to us. That must be a sign. Would you wear it now?"

"I don't know about signs. But I do know that's a pretty ring."

She put it on and modeled her finger for us. Jack was grinning. They seemed stiff when they got up, so I gave Jack his cane and they headed for the bedroom. Their belated joy, the way they hugged, made me smile.

CHAPTER 12

✦

I CLOSED THE BEDROOM DOOR so the dim light of the Tiffany lamp wouldn't disturb their sleep. In the quiet living room, I found the photo album stuck in the sofa cushion and looked, again, at the photo of Dad, Langston, Cousin Ella, and Tyree signing this very contract that I had in hand. Three were reading the papers on the table. Dad, holding a pen, was looking straight at the camera. I sensed he was looking at me, as if he were pleading to make things right between us. His eyes caused me to panic. What was I thinking? Was grief overwhelming my rational thoughts?

I took over an hour to read every page of the condo sale and Tyree Jones's papers. The paperwork for both was in order, with no surprises. I couldn't disqualify one or the other. I set them down in two neat piles on the credenza to review more thoroughly later. I wanted to make an informed decision. Langston's reassuring smile was in front of me.

I had to focus on chores—whatever productive busywork I could do to keep calm. I found the yellow pages and made a list of three possible storage spaces in the Bronx and Manhattan for the contents of the apartment. What I'd do with their property later, I had no idea. But I'd have to choose storage space very early in the morning—before leaving for the lawyer's appointment—so I could tell the mover where to go.

Next, Jack. I couldn't think of anything permanent, but I'd call the YMCA to try to get a room for him. He could afford to pay for that himself and would have other men to talk to.

Cousin Ella. No problem. Her assisted living apartment was ready. But getting her outside for the first time in years—and apart from Jack—could be heartbreaking or, worse, cause her, as frail as she was, to have a heart attack.

And Bill. I'd just remembered that he'd left me two phone messages. I had to listen. I could call him back around seven when he'd be having his morning coffee. The first message was left late afternoon, around the time he should've returned to the condo.

I'd planned to be more social, but I felt weird when I got there, like I'd stepped into an old B movie set.

I could understand that. I'd felt weird, too, at first. When they dressed up for that salon, I was annoyed, but thought it would be interesting. Then it turned painful. I wanted to reach out to them all to let them know how I'd felt, but something held me back. I'd tried to stay businesslike, but couldn't. Do you understand this, Bill? Despite the pain, when they dressed up like that, they made those old clothes live. They were no longer just piles on the floor.

And there you were with those strange looking people who you call your "family."

Really? I don't just call them family. Cousin Ella is family. I can't ignore that.

I was afraid, Carrie. Afraid for you, that something was wrong with you.

Wrong with me? Why? Maybe it was you. You should've just accepted what you saw like I tried to do. Sure, maybe you couldn't. At least I didn't insult them like you did with your rudeness.

And we can't have a team when we have only two players and one is down.

Can't you get it? I didn't sign a contract to be on a team, Bill. I signed the marriage certificate to be your wife. Remember that? We were even lovers—for a while, anyway. I miss that, Bill. I'm tired of feeling like a business partner.

But again, I want you to know that I feel very bad about your dad. He was good to me in a way that my own father wasn't.

I know. We always talked about how you had a single mom and I had a single father. We thought we could put together a semblance of a family. But your mother never seemed to like me. No matter how many promotions I got, I always thought she dismissed me as not ambitious enough for her only son. Have I been good enough, Bill? You never give me a hint that you value me—who I really am—beyond my next paycheck. But Dad? Now I realize I was mistaken when I thought he was more supportive of you than he ever was of me. I couldn't let go of my anger over the audition. I admit I'm still trying to free myself from that. But now I think he might have just figured you'd do well enough to keep me secure. In his way, Bill, when he gave you pep talks, he was really looking out for me.

Carrie, I care about you.

I heard my voice saying I care about you, too. I'm even proud of you. You've done so well for yourself. But isn't it strange that neither of us ever said, "I love you"?

This hurt. I stopped the messages for a moment to breathe.

A moment after I said that out loud, I nearly jumped out of my skin and dropped the phone as hands massaged my shoulders. I turned around in the dim light and saw a spectral figure.

"Carrie, you deserve better."

"Cousin Ella?"

"Who did you think it was?"

"You look . . ."

"Different, yes. I'm ready, Carrie. How do I look?"

She stood back into the light so I could see her better. She was wearing a wrinkled, tailored navy suit—the skirt was long below her knees—and a white ruffled blouse with a pearl necklace. Her feet were in scuffed black tie-up shoes. The hosiery on her stubby legs was faded too light for her skin color and had the

start of a run at the ankle. But it was her face—her
head actually—that stunned me. Her long hair was
neatly combed back into a chignon style. Her face was
perfectly made up. She looked maybe seventy-five, not
ninety-five. She wore a small red hat with a jaunty little
feather and a black veil that she had cleverly arranged
to cover her scar. Where did she get those clothes? I'd
thought all of her things were packed.

She waved her hand with Jack's ring, paused, then
did it again with a flourish, as if she were dancing.

"So, Carrie, how do I look?"

"Good. No, great!"

"These are my going-out clothes. I saved them
because I always knew I'd need them someday. I didn't
think you'd bother to look under the mattress, especially with how the leak messed up the bed. I was
right. I put that red dress there too, after . . . "

"Do you want it?"

"Throw it away. Please. It's over there by the bedroom door. I don't want to touch it more than I need
to."

When I went to put it in the trash bag, the touch
of it sent me to Paris with Cousin Ella. I envisioned
her smiling and happy. I imagined Tyree Jones's young
dancers in red, performing in Paris—or wherever in
the world they wanted to be. I could make that happen. No. I shouldn't be thinking that now. I had to
follow my to-do list.

I picked up and checked the time on my phone. It
was three in the morning.

"Why are you up so early?"

"I'm like you. I couldn't sleep. Too many changes going on. I wanted to be awake in the time I have left in my home."

"And Jack?"

"Him? He could sleep through anything. Don't you hear him snoring?"

"Maybe, I guess." I didn't.

She glanced toward my two stacks of papers. Then, somehow, in the near darkness, she was able to feel through a box of records. She put "God Bless the Child" on the player that was still unpacked. I was compelled to listen to Holiday's every word.

"Dance with me, Carrie."

Cousin Ella was shaking as we danced at arm's length to a slow, scratchy Billie.

While we were dancing, Cousin Ella said, "Langston, you know, helped talented young people—even older ones, like Doyle. He tried to prod Doyle along with his drawing. But Doyle was stubborn—he didn't take the bait. I think Doyle died regretting that."

I suddenly had the memory of Dad's letter.

She has a gift for you. It's something of value that I'm ashamed that I couldn't give you and too afraid to give myself. Carrie, I want to make it right. I want you to be happy.

When it was over, she said, "Wouldn't you have liked to have had someone like Langston help you when you were young and wanted to be a dancer?"

I could only whisper, "Yes."

She nodded and squeezed my hand. Then she went to the sofa and dozed. I mentally repeated Dad's words, then replayed the record and sat on a box in the dark and listened to the song punctuated by Cousin Ella's old lady snores.

I didn't want it to stop, but I had to listen to Bill's second message. It was timed at a few hours later than the first. He formed his words precisely. He was trying to disguise that he'd had wine with his dinner. I knew him too well to be fooled. He couldn't handle one glass. Did he have it with that redhead?

I'm sorry that you didn't see fit to go to the lawyer's today.

I don't like your tone. You saw what I was doing and you knew why I couldn't go. Why didn't you stay to help me since you thought the appointment was so important? I would have gotten to the appointment if you had helped. Do you get that, team player?

Or to even sign the papers that I made the effort to bring to you—with a notary!

Would you sign away your home without reading the fine print? Or sign anything in the middle of a busy sidewalk? No, but you'd have me sign away my condo—my condo that you lived in all these years!

I've made an appointment for you to take care of this at 9:30 in the morning.

That's so helpful of you. You didn't bother to ask what time would be good for me.

Be there! We—me, the buyers, the lawyer—are all being patient with you.

What? So that's it? Everyone has to be patient with me? Look, don't push me! It's something of mine that all of you want. Yeah, be as patient as you like.

But this is it. We'll lose all of it if you don't show.

Lose? You mean lose *my* money? And what do I gain on this team? You know what would be really nice? Show me some love, man. That's all I want.

Oh, and clean yourself up. I've gotta tell you it was hard for me to be next to you in that cluttered up bedroom. You smelled almost as bad as that fetid stairway. And you're sleeping there? I'm sure you'll stink even more.

OK. I don't have water to take a shower. I don't have a change of clothes. I do have two old people who must leave a place and I don't even know if they can walk down the stairs!

But I knew I shouldn't be angry. No, he was right. I had promised him I'd be there. And yes, I was a mess. Cousin Ella looked better than I did. OK. Bill could bring some clothes for me. I could change and quickly wash up in the lawyer's restroom. Then would I be acceptable enough to him to sign away my home? Would I ever be acceptable? Or loveable?

I had to admit that his attitude galled me. I never expected him to ask about me—he always took me for granted—but he never once asked how Cousin Ella and Jack were faring. But, really, I had to look at myself and what I'd done. I'd missed the appointment and hung up on him. What were we doing to each other? Was this a winning team?

Dad, what did you want me to make right?

I was beginning to sense the answer, but I had to deal with today's business. Cousin Ella, sleeping deeply on the sofa, looked frail and tiny in her business suit. I hadn't heard Jack's snoring, which was making me anxious, so I opened the bedroom door to peek in. Wafts of smothering alcohol fumes took my breath away. I heard his quiet breathing and quickly closed the door. Even if I could somehow keep them together in the assisted living apartment, he wouldn't be able to drink as he had. The building's managers had rules to conform to. How would Cousin Ella and Jack—these two still-independent old souls—adjust to living in a place like that?

I was totally fatigued. I gathered up some of the blankets that Zee had left behind to make a pallet for myself next to the sofa. I dozed a bit, but Cousin Ella had been right. There were too many changes going on. As soon as light slanted in through the blinds, I gradually opened my eyes. Langston was still smiling at me. Dad's photo, with the piercing eyes, was propped up next to him. Did I position the photos to face me?

"Good morning!"

Cousin Ella was standing above me with a big smile. Her red hat was tilted. I heard Jack shuffling and mumbling in the bedroom.

"Carrie, come on, get up. Felix brought us coffee and donuts."

I hadn't heard Felix. But I did hear the clanking of the workers' tools on the other side of the hallway. If Felix could keep them from Cousin Ella's door until the afternoon, we'd have time to leave with dignity.

I wondered who would enter the new doors. Would the new young residents sense the ghosts that would always lurk in these rooms? As I glanced around the room, I was overwhelmed by all that had happened there. I would always carry that with me.

"You sure talk a lot in your sleep." Cousin Ella was beaming.

I was afraid to ask what I'd said.

I heard Jack's cane thumping out of the bedroom. When I turned I saw him in yesterday's pinstriped suit with a clean, wrinkled white shirt and navy tie. He had a slightly squashed fedora on his head. I quietly laughed and cried when he walked over to Cousin Ella and kissed her cheek. It looked so easy, as if he did this every morning. It was clear to me that, if they kept nothing else, they deserved to keep their love.

My years with Bill were filled with sameness in the mornings. Rushed cup of coffee, maybe some toast, a yelled list of to-dos—pay the credit card, buy mustard, and the more often "I'll be late"—on the way out of the door. Never that easy kiss on the cheek. Our home routine was similar to Dad's—unchangeable.

I looked around the room at the furniture, boxes, and the few pieces of artwork that had yet to be packed. It would be tight. Much would have to be sold or trashed, but enough could be kept for a comfortable fit in my empty condo. Bill could sell my art collection for the mortgage. Jack and Cousin Ella could sell those diamonds and antiques to support themselves. I'd have to call Bill now, before I changed my mind. It would be difficult, but I had to do it.

ACKNOWLEDGMENTS

THANKS to Steve Eisner for seeing the potential; to Dede Cummings (Green Writers Press, publisher) and Rose Alexandre-Leach (editor) for being supportive and a pleasure to work with; to Jill Norman for bringing the Paul Breman Collection to Chapin Library at Williams College; to Dr. Amritjit Singh, Langston Hughes Professor of English and African American Studies, Emeritus, (Ohio University) for research suggestions; to *Re-Markings* (editor Nibir K. Ghosh) for publishing my Langston poems; to Michael, Jason, Anna, Alice, Alvin, and Joanne for their support; and my special *Dhanyavada* to Chuck for being.

ABOUT THE AUTHOR

SHARYN SKEETER is a writer, poet, editor, and educator. She was fiction/poetry/book review editor at Essence and editor in chief at Black Elegance magazine. She's taught at Emerson College, University of Bridgeport, Fairfield University, and Gateway and Three Rivers community colleges. She participated in panel discussions and readings at universities in India and Singapore. Sharyn Skeeter has published numerous magazine articles. Her poetry and fiction is in journals and anthologies. She lives in Seattle where she's on the board of trustees of ACT Theatre. Her grandmother's Langston family and their oral history of Langston Hughes inspired *Dancing with Langston*.

A Reading and Discussion Group Guide

✦

Here are questions and topics to encourage interesting and enjoyable discussions for reading groups and individuals.

In the novel, Carrie, Doyle, and Langston are faced with choices. Should they be householders with domestic responsibilities or should they follow their talents in the arts? They are also concerned with elder care, gentrification, preservation of history, and human rights. These are blended with Buddhist themes of impermanence, attachment, compassion, suffering, and the alleviation of suffering. In *Dancing with Langston*, Carrie must find a middle way through these challenges, so that she and those she cares about can thrive.

Discussion Questions
- The setting is a building in Harlem that is being gentrified. This is a common occurrence there and elsewhere. Carrie becomes aware of the history

of place that the long-term residents in the neighborhood have created. Whether they stay or leave, how will this change affect those residents?

- From the window, Carrie sees some of the new residents going about their day. What of their historical context and culture do they bring to the neighborhood?
- How do Langston's and Doyle's differences and similarities affect Carrie?
- How are the characters affected by dance? Why is that important?
- Cousin Ella hasn't left her apartment in decades. Langston and Doyle are regular visitors. Carrie doesn't leave for her appointment. Why is the closed world inside the apartment important to Cousin Ella, Langston, Doyle, and later Carrie?
- Carrie has been taught to be loyal to family members. How does she manage this role?
- Cousin Ella calls her possessions her life's history. What is her attitude toward letting them go?
- Zee is often attached to fantasies. What are her unmet needs that might cause this? What happens that gets her to deal with her actual situation?
- Several of the male characters had experienced segregation in the military when they fought in World War II. President Truman desegregated the forces in 1948. How do these men cope with that experience and PTSD in its aftermath?
- How will the younger characters Angel and Jimmy experience life differently from their elders? What

will the older generation transmit to the young people?

- Carrie learns to love her father after he died. Why? Was there any way she could have done this before his death? What has she learned from this?
- What are Cousin Ella's, Langston's, and Doyle's motivations for giving Carrie the gift? They did this together. Why is that significant in Carrie's final decision?
- Why does Jack drink and keep the monkey doll?
- Cousin Ella had a positive attitude when she was a young woman. How and why has Cousin Ella deprived herself of later happiness? At ninety-five, is there a chance for her to be happy?
- Why did Carrie marry Bill? How has that decision influenced other areas of her life?
- What does Carrie's imaginary conversation with Bill's voicemail reveal about her character by the end of the novel?
- Cousin Ella and Jack's relationship is complicated, full of love but also regret, guilt, and resentment. How do you think they were able to stay together as long as they have despite all of these emotions and their complex history?
- How do Cousin Ella and Carrie's relationships with their significant others compare to one another?
- What roles do Angel and Jimmy Two-Cent play in the small world of Cousin Ella and Jack?
- Jack says that Cousin Ella enjoys the company of younger men like Felix, yet she doesn't show the same interest in Jimmy-Two Cent. She also had

good friendships with cousins Langston in Paris and Doyle in New York City. Besides age, does Cousin Ella think they have characteristics that Jack doesn't? How does she find happiness with Jack?

More Topics
- Look up the Buddhist Four Noble Truths and use them to analyze the characters' development. A good place to find this would be buddhanet.net.
- If you are not familiar with the work of the real, highly prolific American author Langston Hughes, look up his work and read what you like—poetry, memoirs, articles, plays, translations, letters, short stories.
- Enjoy listening to the music mentioned in book. It's available on YouTube and many other sites. Consider what this music might say about the characters.
- Become familiar with the artists' early works that Cousin Ella collected: Romare Bearden, Lois Maillou Jones, Jacob Lawrence, James VanDerZee, and others.
- Learn about performers like Josephine Baker, Bricktop, Sammy Davis, Jr., Cab Calloway, and Katherine Dunham.

A NOTE ON THE TYPE

Dancing With Langston was typeset in Dante. The first Dante fonts were the result of a collaboration between two exceptional men. One was Giovanni Mardersteig, a printer, book designer and typeface artist of remarkable skill and taste who was renowned for the work he produced at Officina Bodoni and Stamperia Valdònega, his two printing offices in Italy. The other was Charles Malin, one of the great punch-cutters of the twentieth century.

As a young man at the turn of the last century, Mardersteig developed a keen interest in the typefaces and printing of Giambattista Bodoni. He was fortunate enough to obtain permission to use Bodoni's original types, for which punches and matrices were still preserved. Charles Malin cut replacements for some of these original punches, and later cut punches for nearly all the new typefaces Mardersteig created.

Dante was Mardersteig's last and most successful design. By then he had gained a deep knowledge of what makes a typeface lively, legible, and handsome. Working closely with Malin had also taught him the nuances of letterform construction. For Dante, the two worked closely to develop a design that was easy to read. For example, special care was taken with the design of the serifs and top curves of the lowercase to create a subtle horizontal stress, which helps the eye move smoothly across the page. After six years of work, the fonts were first used in 1955 to publish Boccaccio's *Trattatello in Laude di Dante*—hence the typeface name.

·❖·

DESIGN BY DEDE CUMMINGS

BRATTLEBORO, VERMONT